Hi, I'm Jodie Ounsley and I'm so glad you picked up my book.

You might know me as Fury from the TV show *Gladiators*. Or you might like rugby and maybe you know me from when I played for England and Great Britain. Or you might have seen some of the work I do telling people what it's like to live as a profoundly deaf person. You might not know me at all, and if that's the case, it's lovely to meet you. I'm really excited to share some stories from my life with you.

My life hasn't turned out at all how I'd expected but I have learned some really great things along the way. I hope that this book will help you feel **stronger, braver** and **more confident.**

You're already smashing life, and I want to help you to keep smashing it as you continue on your amazing journey.

I want to say, right at the start, that **I don't have all the answers.** My life has not been perfect. There have been twists, turns and disappointments. There have been times when I wanted to give up. When I found it hard to believe in myself. When everything just felt too difficult.

But I've also learned how to say **YES** to the things that scare me. I've learned that sometimes taking a big, scary leap into the unknown can bring opportunities you would never have expected for yourself. I've learned how to adapt and get around barriers, even when things have seemed impossible. **I want to share all of these amazing moments with you, in case what I've**

KEEP SMASHING IT

★ ★

BE STRONG
BE BRAVE
BE CONFIDENT

JODIE OUNSLEY

KEEP SMASHING IT

BE STRONG
BE BRAVE
BE CONFIDENT

Written with Becky Grey

MACMILLAN CHILDREN'S BOOKS

Published 2025 by Macmillan Children's Books,
an imprint of Pan Macmillan
The Smithson, 6 Briset Street, London EC1M 5NR
EU representative: Macmillan Publishers Ireland Ltd, 1st Floor,
The Liffey Trust Centre, 117–126 Sheriff Street Upper
Dublin 1, D01 YC43
Associated companies throughout the world
www.panmacmillan.com

ISBN 978-1-0350-6404-5

Text copyright © Jodie Ounsley 2025
BSL Illustrations copyright © Dane Thibeault 2025

The right of Jodie Ounsley and Dane Thibeault to be identified as the
author and illustrator of this work has been asserted by them in
accordance with the Copyright, Designs and Patents Act 1988.

3 5 7 9 8 6 4

A CIP catalogue record for this book is available from the British Library.

Printed and bound by CPI Group (UK) Ltd, Croydon CR0 4YY
Interior design by Janene Spencer

I dedicate this book to all those amazing kids out there – believe in yourselves and chase your dreams.

Be proud to be unique. Be proud to be you. Walk out of that door everyday with a big smile and go and smash life!

CONTENTS

learned can help you. One of the most important things I've learned so far is that . . .

LIFE ISN'T ALWAYS GOING TO BE PERFECT. AND THAT'S OKAY.

Things go wrong and that is absolutely fine. In fact, it's part of life.

Sometimes, when people see a sportsperson or any person who they think is successful – for example, someone on TV like me – they assume that their life is amazing. That it's always been easy for them. That they haven't had to work hard to achieve that success.

It's easy to think that, because you tend to only see the successes in people's lives.

But guess what? **That's not true.**

In this book, I want to be honest about the ups and downs of my life. I hope that sharing my stories will help you feel less alone in any struggles that you're facing.

I didn't have the easiest start to life. Not long after I was born, my parents found out I was profoundly deaf. That means I don't have any hearing in either of my ears. My mum and dad were told I would probably never be able to speak, that I wouldn't be able to get an education, and that I was unlikely to get a job, either. Well, I made it through school and **now I have one of the best jobs in the world – smashing people on TV as a Gladiator.** Not only can I speak, I use my voice to tell people what it's like to be deaf. I get to be a role model for deaf people all over the world. And I often have to stand on big stages in front of large audiences – which can sometimes be really scary! – but I love doing it.

To get to where I am today and **smash the limits** that other people set for me, the most important thing I had to do was believe in myself.

It would make me really happy if, after reading this book, you were able to believe in yourself too.

> I'VE DONE A LOT OF THINGS IN MY LIFE THAT HAVE SCARED ME. BUT I BELIEVE THAT WHEN WE PUSH OURSELVES OUT OF OUR COMFORT ZONES, WE GET SOME OF OUR BIGGEST WINS.

I was really nervous when I first tried rugby and when I applied to be on *Gladiators*. I wasn't sure if it was something I should do, and it was definitely outside of my comfort zone. But it's one of the best decisions I have ever made. It's given me so many amazing opportunities.

I want you to push your limits beyond what you thought was possible. To go for the things that make you happy. I want you to be brave and know that when an opportunity comes your way, you are strong enough to give it a go, even if it's scary. I hope this book, and the things I'm going to share with you, can help you to do that. I've included some questions for you at the end of each chapter, which I hope can get you thinking about what I've shared.

There's also a chance for you to learn some British Sign Language, which is a language used by some people in the deaf community. In British Sign Language, or BSL, people use their hands and body to communicate. You might already use BSL, but if you're new to it there are illustrations at the start of each chapter to show you how to say the chapter title in BSL and the BSL alphabet is included at the back of the book too. Notice how the words are sometimes in a different order from English – BSL has its own grammar and the order of the signs is important.

In this book I'm going to talk a lot about the three things I believe in most:

BEING KIND

WORKING HARD

MAKING A DIFFERENCE

Even when things have been confusing, worrying or scary, sticking to those three beliefs has seen me right. I am driven by my passions and can be quite fiery too – you might have noticed that if you've seen me on a rugby pitch or you watch *Gladiators*! – and I have always had a drive to do good in the world. I grew up with strong role models, but none of them were deaf, so I'm very passionate about being that person to others.

I want to share the experiences I've struggled with and the things that have helped me through tough times. It might be that one of the struggles I've had in my life is something you've experienced. Or maybe you've been in a similar situation, or know someone who's struggling. I hope that by reading about my life you can learn how to help yourself and those around you.

I'm also going to talk about how I found a passion that makes me happy. I'll explain how I learned that sometimes things change and that's okay. I'll tell you about times in my life when I've found it hard to be myself, and how I came to understand that everything is just so much easier when I'm honest about who I am and what I need help with.

I'LL WARN YOU NOW: there is a lot of love for my parents in these pages. They have been a huge support to me and I want to help you find the best people to support you when things are hard in your life.

I joke with my family that if we looked back to before I got involved with *Gladiators*, or before my rugby career, we would never have expected my life to be what it is now.

In fact, the life I have still feels mind-blowing to me. I'm going to be cheesy for a second: I feel really lucky.

If you take nothing else away from reading this, please remember: **I want you to back yourself.**

Learning to back myself has brought me some pretty special things, and you deserve to believe in yourself and be the best you can be too.

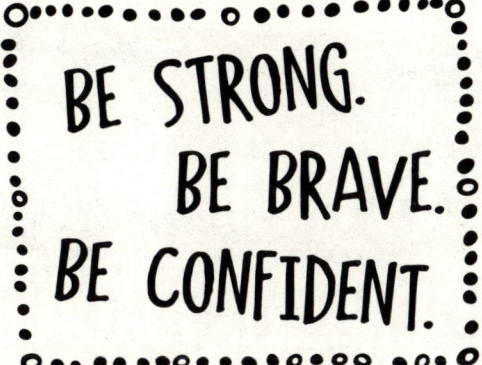

BE STRONG.
BE BRAVE.
BE CONFIDENT.

Keep smashing it,
Jodie

CHAPTER 1

WHAT IS YOUR DREAM?

DREAM

YOUR

WHAT?

I want to talk to you about dreams.

For a long time, I knew what my dream was – I wanted to be an Olympian. I didn't know what sport  I was going to do; I just knew that I wanted to compete at the Olympics, in any way possible.

My dream was born when I first watched the Olympics on TV, aged seven. It was the 2008 Games in Beijing. We were getting ready to watch the final of the men's 100-metre race, and my mum told me that we were about to see the fastest man in the world compete.

At the time I didn't know who he was, but I still remember how amazing it was to watch him in that race. He was so relaxed. As he got near the finish line it was clear that he was going to win – and he even slowed down to celebrate! And he STILL set a new world record! It was so inspiring to watch.

His name was Usain Bolt. You might not have heard of him, but he was the best sprinter in the world when I was growing up. He won gold medals in the 100-metre and 200-metre sprints that year, and then won another six gold medals at two more Olympic Games, in 2012 and 2016. He is an incredible athlete.

See if you can watch some of his races. I think you'll understand why I was so impressed by him!

From that moment, I was obsessed with the Olympics. I just had this really strong feeling that *that* was where I needed to be. I had always loved playing sports, but after watching Usain Bolt win that race, I knew I wanted to compete at an Olympic Games.

Growing up, I always loved PE at school. Being deaf made some of my other classes challenging – I couldn't always hear what the teacher or my classmates were saying – but it wasn't like that in PE. In PE, I could forget about all that and just have fun because I felt like I belonged. And, of course, I knew being good at PE was the first tiny step on my journey to the Olympics.

OLYMPICS: The biggest sporting event in the world, which takes place every four years. Athletes from more than 200 countries compete in around thirty different sports. There are Summer Olympics, with summer sports, and the Winter Olympics, with winter sports – which always happen two years after the Summer Olympics. So you get to see an Olympic Games of some sort every two years!

PARALYMPICS: The biggest disability sporting event in the world, with around 170 countries competing in about twenty sports. The Paralympics take place immediately after the Olympics and there are both Summer Paralympics and Winter Paralympics, too.

The next Summer Olympics and Paralympics after Beijing was London 2012. Having the Games in Great Britain was amazing. It seemed as if everyone, across the whole country, was *obsessed* with them. Everywhere you looked, the Games were staring back at you. It was all we could talk about at school; London 2012 was on adverts, toys, food, drink – everything! The whole country seemed to stop for a month to watch every minute they could on TV.

At the London 2012 Olympics there was this amazing athlete called Jessica Ennis-Hill, who won a gold medal. She did heptathlon, where you do seven different athletics events over two days. On the first day of the event she took part in the 100-metre hurdles, high jump, shot put and the 200-metre sprint. On the second day she did long jump and javelin throw, then

finished by winning the 800-metre race with a whole stadium full of people screaming in support. It looked exhausting, and I found it so inspiring.

Following in hers and Usain Bolt's footsteps, the first thing I focused on to try to make my Olympic dream happen was athletics.

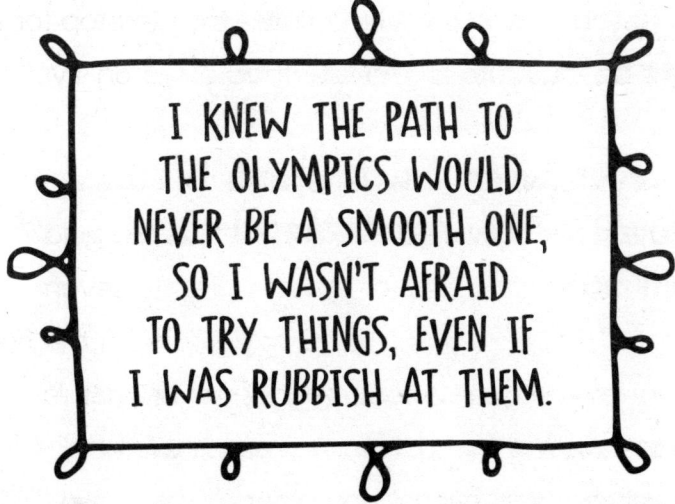

I KNEW THE PATH TO THE OLYMPICS WOULD NEVER BE A SMOOTH ONE, SO I WASN'T AFRAID TO TRY THINGS, EVEN IF I WAS RUBBISH AT THEM.

First, I tried long jump. I soon gave that up, though — turns out I wasn't great at it! I gave discus a go, too. (That's where you throw a weight that is shaped like a disc and see how far it will go.) But again, I quickly realized that wasn't the event for me! I was good at running fast, so eventually I took up sprinting. That was especially fun, as I was best at the 100 metres and 200 metres, like Usain Bolt. When I was nine I started to take part in competitions, and for a long time I thought athletics might be my route to the Olympics.

However, when I was about fifteen I found a new sport that I loved even more.

That was the year when my younger brother Jack started playing rugby. I didn't really know what it was at the time, but when I went to watch him play it looked amazing. So fun and so physical. I was desperate to get on the pitch and get involved. I just had this feeling that I'd be really good at it. I thought that my speed, which made me good at running in track sports, would help with rugby. In athletics, I was always competing on my own and I loved the idea of playing rugby as part of a team. I'll be honest, the way people got to smash into each other looked very fun too!

And once I'd played my first game of rugby, I instantly felt like I belonged on the pitch.

Then, to top it all off, I found out that rugby was going to be included in the Olympics for the first time at the 2016 Summer Games in Rio.

I couldn't believe it. My new passion could help me get to the Olympics! By focusing on what I found fun and what made me happy, I'd moved a step closer to realizing my dream.

When I started playing rugby, all I knew was that you could only pass the ball backwards. But even though I didn't know much, after my first training session I was asked to be in the squad for my local team. Within a couple of months I'd started playing for my county team, Yorkshire, which was more competitive.

I wanted to do everything I could to get into the England Sevens team.

Sevens is the type of rugby they play in the Olympics — there are seven players on each team and it is a much faster form of the game. (There's also 15-a-side rugby, which has fifteen players on each team. With this number of players, the game is a bit slower and more physical.)

I hoped that if I played for England Sevens I would be picked for the Great Britain team that would go to the Olympics. And, in 2019, when I was eighteen years old, I played for England for the first time, just three years after I had started playing rugby. I'd managed to make sport my job and I was travelling the world doing it. It was an incredible time in my life.

Having one dream that I was so focused on was really useful for me. It gave me something that I could always work towards, and that's how I got to play for England so soon after starting rugby. I knew what I wanted and I worked hard to get it.

WHEN I WAS STRUGGLING IN A TOUGH TRAINING SESSION OR HAVING A DIFFICULT TIME ON THE PITCH, I JUST HAD TO THINK ABOUT THE REASON WHY I WAS DOING IT.
I WANTED TO GET TO THE OLYMPICS.

Do you have a dream? If you do, that's amazing. Having a clear dream can be really helpful. It can inspire you to work hard and give you focus in your life. But, at the same time, if you're not sure what your dream is yet, that's okay.

> JUST THINK ABOUT
> WHAT MAKES YOU HAPPY
> AND MAKE SURE YOU'RE DOING THAT.
> A DREAM MIGHT COME FROM IT.

If you choose a really big dream, sometimes people might worry that it's too difficult to achieve. I knew I wanted to be a sportsperson when I grew up, but some of my teachers told me it wasn't a realistic choice. I knew becoming an Olympian would be really, really hard, but I also knew it would make me happy and I at least wanted to try!

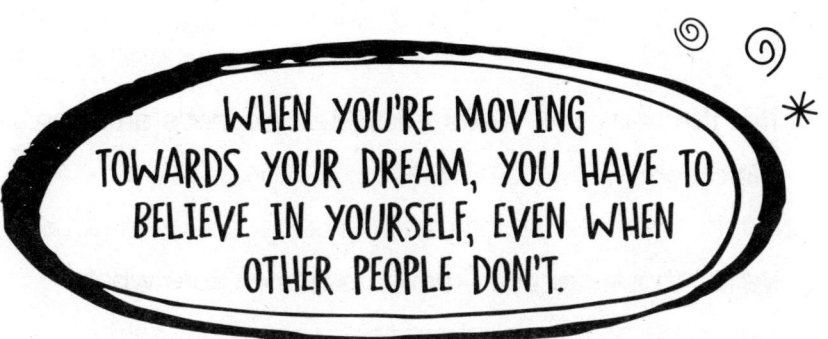

WHEN YOU'RE MOVING TOWARDS YOUR DREAM, YOU HAVE TO BELIEVE IN YOURSELF, EVEN WHEN OTHER PEOPLE DON'T.

If you know what your dream is, follow it. Don't let other people tell you that you can't even try.

When you have a goal, it can help to write it down so it feels more real. I used to have a whiteboard in my room with the words 'Compete at the Olympics' written on it in big letters. It was the last thing I saw at night before going to sleep and the first thing I saw when I woke up in the morning. Writing it down kept me focused.

'COMPETE AT THE OLYMPICS'

Of course, having such a big dream also made me worry sometimes. I would think things like,

What if I don't get there?

Am I being silly?

What if I'm not good enough to be there?

Am I dreaming too big?

25

But the truth is, it takes a lot of strength to have a big dream.

When those negative thoughts come up, it can be helpful to focus on smaller, more manageable steps. I also used to write down smaller goals on my whiteboard: achievable, everyday things that would help me get to the Olympics.

For example, I knew I needed to get picked for the Great Britain Sevens squad.

To do that, I needed to play well for England at tournaments, so that the Great Britain coaches would notice me.

And to be able to play well for England, I had to work hard in training. So my smaller goal would be:

'TRY YOUR BEST IN TRAINING.'

Breaking down larger goals into smaller steps is so important when you're chasing a dream.

Having a target helped me make decisions, too. If I wasn't sure what was the right thing to do, I could just think, 'Is this going to help me get to the Olympics?' I would try anything to get there, even stuff I wasn't good at (like discus!), and even though they turned out not to be the right step, I had a lot of fun doing them. It also really helped me feel confident about being different when other people at school weren't as interested in sport as me. **I knew what I wanted to do and I didn't want to apologize for that.**

I know not everyone is clear about what their dream is, but don't let that worry you. What's important is that you do things that genuinely make you happy. Your thing might be a sport, it could be painting or drawing, making things, singing or a certain subject at school. **If you concentrate on what makes you happy, good things will come from that.** You might even find yourself in situations that you would never have dreamed of!

That's what has happened to me. I don't play rugby any more and I don't know what my end goal is, but I love what I'm doing and it's opening doors that I would never have even thought to try to open.

It won't always be easy. If you do find your dream, trying to chase it can feel like a lot of work. When that happens, break down your dream into small steps.

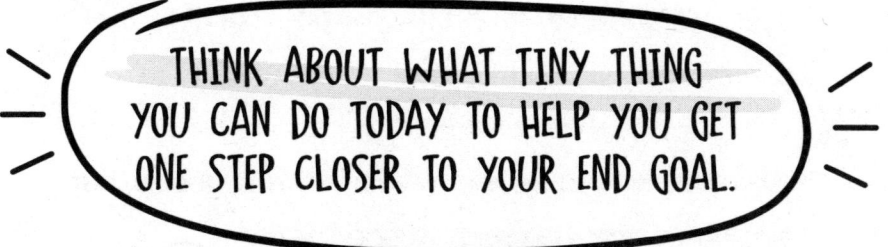

THINK ABOUT WHAT TINY THING YOU CAN DO TODAY TO HELP YOU GET ONE STEP CLOSER TO YOUR END GOAL.

You don't have to make your dream happen overnight, and sometimes you might get tired and need to take a break. That's okay too. Once you've had a rest, focus your energy back on the things that you are passionate about; doing that will help you work out what is best for you.

ACTIVITIES

Here are a few questions and prompts to get you thinking about dreams.

It might be nice to have a notebook and pen nearby, because writing things out while you think about them can be helpful. Personally, I like a spider diagram, especially when I can make them colourful. Spider diagrams help me expand on my thoughts and see how everything connects together.

If that's not for you, you can think through your answers by talking out loud. Or you can just have a quiet think in your head.

If you don't know the answer to some of the questions, that's okay. Let them sit in your brain and a solution might come to you later.

To find my dream, I focused on things that made me happy, like playing sport.

1 **Close your eyes and take three deep breaths. Imagine you are doing something that makes you feel really happy. Now write down or say out loud what that thing was.**

2 **As well as making you feel happy, your dream might be something you feel really strongly about. What are the things you really care about? You might be like me and think sport is really important. Or, the thing that gets you excited could be music, or reading a new book!**

3 Now that you have thought about what makes you feel happy and what you care about, is there anything new you'd like to try?

4 Do you have a dream? If so, what is it?

5 Can you think of four small steps that you can take to get you closer to your dream? For example, if your dream involves sport, you could do some research about local sports clubs. You could plan to do more training in your sport, or get some advice from someone else who plays the same sport as you.

CHAPTER 2

DREAMS CAN CHANGE

DREAMS

CAN

CHANGE

Let's get something out of the way straight away:
I never did get to play rugby at the Olympics. And
guess what? **That's okay.**

I still find that last part a bit surprising.

 For my whole life, up until I was twenty-two,
all I ever wanted to do was compete at an
Olympic Games. **That was my dream.**
But it's not any more.

One of the biggest things I've learned in my life so
far is that **we are constantly changing and
growing.** You might have noticed this in your life
too. Maybe there's something you were obsessed
with last year — like a sport or a TV programme —
that you're just not that bothered about any more.

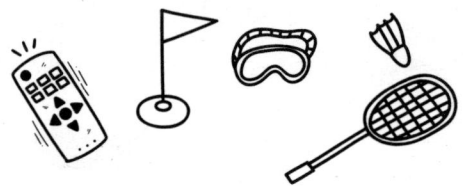

As kids, we're often asked what we want to be when we grow up. You might have the answer to that question already, or you might not. Either way, it's okay. **And it's definitely okay if, one day, you change your mind.** It's great to have a dream for your future, but if you start to feel like that dream isn't right for you any more, you can let it go and find a new one.

One thing I should warn you about, though – when you decide that what you want in your life has changed, it might not be easy. But the end of one dream sometimes means the start of another. And that can be an amazing thing.

So here's how my dream to be in the Olympics ended.

At the start of 2020, I felt excited about my chances of getting selected for the Olympic Games in Tokyo that summer. Five months before the Games were due to begin, I was part of Great Britain's rugby sevens team. It wasn't the final team that would get to go to the Olympics – there were twenty-four of us in the group and only the best thirteen players would get picked for Tokyo – but I was hopeful.

However, as the year went on there was some uncertainty around whether the Games would go ahead because of the coronavirus. This was the virus that caused the whole world to go into lockdown in 2020. The organizers of the Olympics were worried that if people travelled from all over the world to Tokyo, a lot of people would get this virus and be very ill. And, a month after I was picked to be part of the Great Britain team, I found out that the Games were postponed. The Olympics would now take place in 2021, and I had to wait another whole year for my chance. It was frustrating, but it was out of my control, and **I was still confident that I had a good chance of getting into the team.**

While we were waiting to see what would happen with the Olympics, I joined a 15-a-side rugby club called Sale Sharks. During a training session with them in September 2020, I injured myself badly. I was sprinting and I felt something start to hurt in my leg. Afterwards I found out that I had injured my hamstring, which is a muscle in the back of our legs. It should have taken just ten days to recover, but I thought I was fine to do more training. I think playing again too soon after the injury ended up making it much worse; I had to take six months off from playing rugby. By the time the coaches chose the squad for the Olympic Games in 2021, I hadn't played enough. I wasn't picked for the team.

I was only twenty years old and I was completely heartbroken.

For as long as I could remember I had dreamed of going to the Olympics. I wouldn't have another chance for another three whole years . . . My dream wasn't coming true, and one of the hardest things to understand was that it was because of things that were out of my control. If the Olympics hadn't been postponed because of the coronavirus pandemic, or if I hadn't got injured when I did, maybe my dream **would** have come true. Maybe I would have made it to Tokyo.

I had worked so hard and come so close,

but there was nothing more I could have done to make it into the team.

If you've ever experienced something like that in your life, I'm sorry. It's really painful when you want something so much, when you come so close, but you *just* miss out. When that happens you have to give yourself time to be sad about it. **I am a big believer in working hard and trying again,** but I have also learned that when you are dealt a big blow you need to give yourself some time to recover from it.

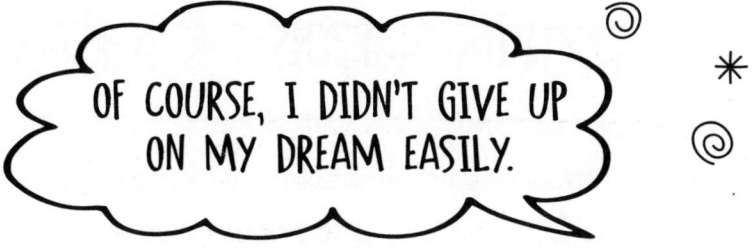

OF COURSE, I DIDN'T GIVE UP ON MY DREAM EASILY.

Eventually, I set my sights on the Paris Olympics in 2024. I worked hard for another year, I gave it my all, but in 2022 my sevens coaches told me that my contract with the team was coming to an end. I would be invited to training camps sometimes, but I knew I wanted to give something my full focus, instead of going to a camp every now and again.

I was devastated all over again. It felt like everything I'd ever wanted, everything I'd been working towards my whole life, was slipping away. For a while, I felt completely lost.

In my house when I was growing up, there were a few sayings we lived by. One of them is:

EVERYTHING HAPPENS FOR A REASON.

I was emotionally drained by the end of my Olympic journey, but I also knew I was in control of what I did next. I could sit in my disappointment and frustration forever, or I could take action. **I could control how I saw the situation and try to look at the heartbreak as an opportunity.** If everything happens for a reason, then I had to try to see that missing out on selection for the Olympics was an opportunity –

I just had to find out what that opportunity was.

I'd had my chance in sevens. I had tried. I had trained hard. I had travelled the world playing for my country, made amazing memories and met incredible people. I had given it my all. But I had always fallen short of the Olympics. It was painful, so painful, but once that pain had subsided a bit, it felt like maybe I was being pointed towards a new challenge.

THIS WAY

So, I started to look forward.

I realized that I had to grab opportunities where I could, even if those opportunities might not take me to the Olympics. And, just a year after I didn't make it to the Tokyo Olympics, a woman called Susie Appleby, who was the head coach of a 15-a-side rugby team called Exeter Chiefs, got in contact.

We started talking about whether I could join her team. I really wanted to find a way to keep playing rugby, and I was so grateful that Susie was offering me that, but it was still a really tough decision. Joining Chiefs would be a new adventure for me, but it would mean that my Olympic dream was truly over, as 15-a-side rugby isn't played at the Olympics, only rugby sevens is. So joining Exeter was a step away from the Games.

When I was thinking about whether to accept the invitation to play for Chiefs, I kept thinking about the phrase 'everything happens for a reason'. It was a scary decision; going into a 15-a-side rugby team would be a big change in my life, but at the same time it was a new challenge that excited me.

Looking back, joining Exeter Chiefs was one of the best decisions I've ever made. **There's no way I'd be where I am in my life** – there's no way I'd be Fury on *Gladiators*! – if I had stayed focused on that Olympic dream and carried on playing sevens.

Moving to Exeter helped me to realize that there was more to life than the Olympics. It even helped me to realize that there was more to life than rugby.

I loved living with my teammates near the beach.

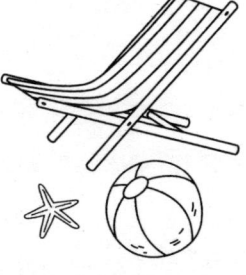

I enjoyed going for coffee with them and generally slowing down, taking one day at a time. I was able to just enjoy playing rugby and the friendships I was building along the way. I started to find smaller, more manageable goals I could aim for. For example, because rugby is a physical sport, I was injured a lot, so even just being able to run out onto the pitch and play on match days started to feel like a win to me.

I enjoyed the little things in life rather than being so hard on myself all the time to achieve this one big goal. It was scary to let go of my Olympic dream, but eventually I started to see that **sometimes things that feel bad at first have actually happened for a reason.** So now when bad things happen, I've learned to be open to the opportunities that might come from them.

I learned that when *Gladiators* unexpectedly came back into my life.

Gladiators is a show that was first on TV in the 1990s, before I was born, but I was a huge fan because my dad had been on a remake of it as a contender in 2009. I was seven when

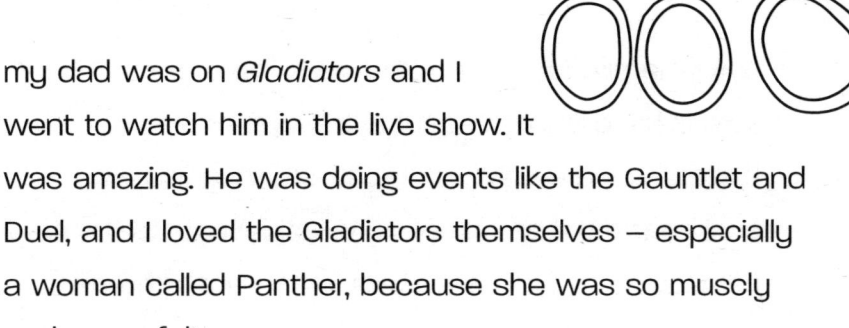

my dad was on *Gladiators* and I
went to watch him in the live show. It
was amazing. He was doing events like the Gauntlet and
Duel, and I loved the Gladiators themselves – especially
a woman called Panther, because she was so muscly
and powerful!

After seeing my dad in action, I loved *Gladiators* so
much that I used to do the training with him at home.
We even had some rings set up in a barn for me to
practise swinging on!

Back when I was still playing sevens I'd heard that
Gladiators was making a comeback, and in 2022 I saw
that applications to actually BE a Gladiator were open.

I COULDN'T BELIEVE IT.

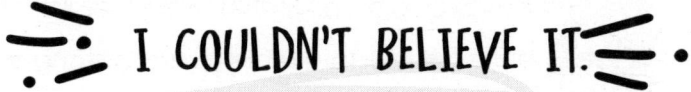

When I was a kid the Gladiators had been like
superheroes to me, so it was hard to believe that

I might actually get the chance to be one.
I decided to apply because the events on
the show were right up my street: they involved
a lot of the things I love – like smashing into things,
competing, running and swinging through the air.

As my Olympic dream was on hold, I thought I might as
well apply – I never thought anything would come of it.

When I got an email inviting me to go to a *Gladiators*
trial, I thought it was fake at first! I didn't seriously think
I was in with a chance, I'd just thought that
it would be fun to apply. So when that email
arrived, I had a hard time believing any of it was real.
It seemed too good to be true.

It was really hard for me to find time around my rugby
commitments, but eventually I travelled to London
for the trial. I had done trials before to get into rugby
teams, but this was so much more intense. There were

different tests to measure our abilities — like **speed,** **strength** and **power.** We had to do things like pull-ups, tackling, jumping up on boxes, rope climbs, burpees and hanging on a bar for as long as you could (which is a lot tougher than it sounds!). It was really, physically tough. Tougher than I expected.

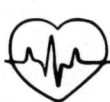

I told them why I wanted to be a Gladiator. Obviously a big part of it was how fun it would be, but **it's always been really important to me to be a good role model for people,** and I could see that *Gladiators* would help to give me a platform for that work.

Eventually, I found out that I was going to be a Gladiator called Fury. I couldn't believe it! It was SO exciting. But I was also really nervous — it was all completely new to me. I wondered,

WHAT IF I GET IT WRONG? WHAT IF I DON'T KNOW WHAT I'M DOING?

I knew I had a lot to learn, and I was also worried about whether it would mean I had to give up rugby. At that time, I wasn't sure if that was something I was prepared to do.

When a new opportunity comes along, particularly one that will change your life, it can feel stressful to try to work out the right decision to make. But I'll let you in on a secret — often, there is no right answer.

YOU CAN ONLY MAKE THE DECISION THAT FEELS BEST TO YOU AT THE TIME.

If you decide to go for something, it's up to you to make it work for you.

That can be really tough, though, so if I need help deciding whether to say yes or no, I ask myself three things:

WILL I BE HAPPY DOING IT?

IS IT SOMETHING THAT MATTERS TO ME?

DOES IT EXCITE ME?

I knew I would be happy doing *Gladiators* because of how fun the events were. I was excited to have the chance to compete in front of such a big audience. And I would have the opportunity to talk about what it's like to be deaf, which mattered a lot to me. So *Gladiators* was **A BIG YES** to all three of those questions.

It can be hard to push yourself out of your comfort zone. It can be scary to try something new, but **saying yes to the things that scare you can lead to amazing things.** If you scare yourself a little bit every day by trying something new, eventually you will feel comfortable doing that thing. Then you can find something else scary to have a go at, and eventually you'll feel comfortable doing that too. That is how our comfort zone grows.

YOU HAVE TO BELIEVE YOU CAN DO SCARY THINGS.

If you believe in yourself, you won't automatically always get what you want. **But if you don't even try, you definitely won't get what you want.** I decided to give *Gladiators* a go, and it completely changed my life.

As soon as I said yes to being a Gladiator, I knew that I'd found my new dream. It's a dream that I never would have had if I had made it to the Olympic Games, so it just goes to show that **amazing things can come out of bad situations.**

In January 2024, *Gladiators* came out on TV. **I was really nervous of what people would think,** but it has brought me loads of new opportunities because it was the first time people outside the world of rugby got to know me. I threw myself into those opportunities, getting more chances to work with new people and meet kids who had been inspired by Fury.

I GOT MYSELF OUT OF MY COMFORT ZONE AND PUSHED MYSELF TO TRY THINGS THAT SCARED ME.

I did more school visits to try to inspire kids with my story. I spoke to big rooms full of people about my experience as a deaf sportsperson. I even started co-hosting a podcast called *Stronger Than You Think*, where we talk to sportswomen about difficult things they've overcome in their lives – and hosting a podcast was something I never thought I'd be able to do! I used to be really shy and didn't feel confident talking to people, so doing it as a job is not something I expected from my life.

The more I did this kind of work, the more I got out of my comfort zone and the more I realized I really enjoyed it. **I felt like there was a fire inside me**. I was getting to meet more and more people thanks to *Gladiators*, and I wanted to use those opportunities to inspire people and teach them about life as a deaf person.

It wasn't all easy. Saying yes to being on *Gladiators* meant I have had to step away from rugby. Rugby had been my whole life; leaving it felt like such a big, scary jump. But my coach at Exeter was so supportive – she told me I had to take opportunities where I could.

One thing I've learned through all of this is that people change. AND CHANGE CAN BE AMAZING IF YOU EMBRACE IT.

Maybe hearing about the end of my Olympic dream has made you think about something you wanted that you couldn't get. Maybe you're sporty like me and you didn't get picked for a sports team. You might be musical, but you didn't get chosen for a certain performance. It might be that you tried really hard for a test at school and didn't get the result you wanted.

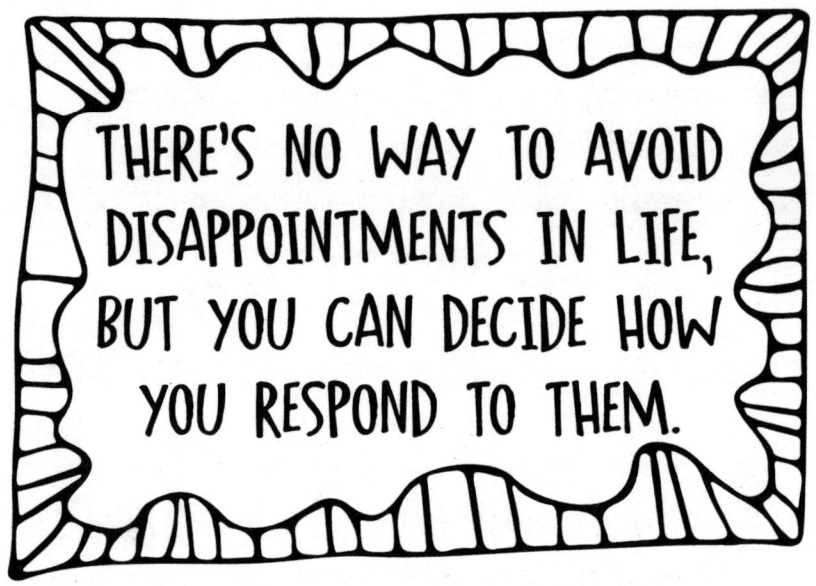

THERE'S NO WAY TO AVOID DISAPPOINTMENTS IN LIFE, BUT YOU CAN DECIDE HOW YOU RESPOND TO THEM.

I stuck with my motto that **everything happens for a reason,** and that meant I looked for new opportunities that could come out of my disappointment. You can plan for what you want your life to be, but some of the best things in life come as a surprise. When something happens that you find tough to take, give yourself time to recover from it. Then, believe that something else will come your way. Look for any opportunities that might be open to you, then when they come, take them.

KNOW THAT I AM BACKING YOU – AND YOU SHOULD BACK YOURSELF.

When I didn't make it to the Olympics, I felt like a failure. Writing that now, it seems so daft, but that's how I saw it at the time.

Our lives are constantly changing, and we have to move and adapt with those changes – I'm not the same person I was in 2020, just as you're not the same person you were yesterday. Deciding what you want in life, and having that dream change, doesn't make you a failure. Living through that makes you strong.

YOUR LIFE ISN'T DEFINED BY THE THINGS YOU DO AND DON'T ACHIEVE; THE MOST IMPORTANT THING IS THAT YOU TRY AND GIVE IT YOUR ALL.

I did everything I could to make my Olympic dream happen, and I'm so proud of myself for trying. I'm proud of you for all the work you've already done to achieve your dream, and I'll be proud if you one day decide to let go of that dream, like I did.

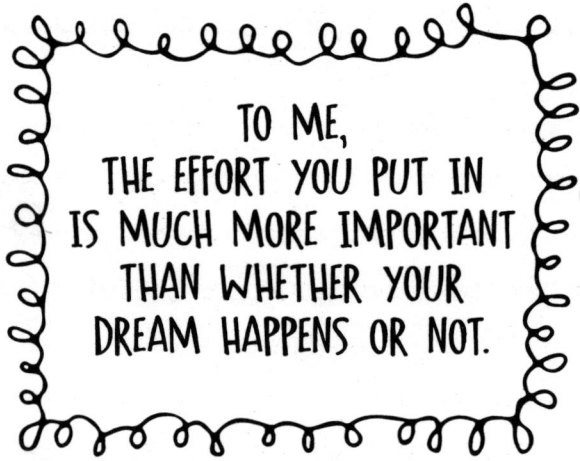

TO ME,
THE EFFORT YOU PUT IN
IS MUCH MORE IMPORTANT
THAN WHETHER YOUR
DREAM HAPPENS OR NOT.

Life is not about having one goal and one route to get to that goal. It's about being open to all the paths in front of us. It's about choosing which one to take depending on what feels best in the moment, and trusting that we will take ourselves in the right direction.

> Sometimes you have to take those BIG JUMPS because what's on the other side can be so much better than what you're leaving behind.

The amazing thing is, in a way, I did almost make it to an Olympic Games. I didn't compete, but because of all the TV work I started doing after *Gladiators* came out, I was asked to be part of Channel 4's presenting team at the 2024 Paralympics.

It felt so right for me. I am so passionate about advocating for disabled people in sport and I got to be part of one of the biggest sporting events in the world.

In a way, it was a dream come true.

* ⊚ * c ♡ *

ACTIVITIES

Here are some questions to get you thinking about what I've talked about in this chapter.

It might help you think if you write down the answers in a notebook, create a spider diagram, talk through them with someone you trust, or just give yourself some quiet time to think about them in your head.

1 Not all bad things lead to good opportunities, but sometimes they do. Think about a time when something hasn't gone the way you wanted it to. Can you think of any opportunities that could have come from that? An example might be that you didn't get picked for a sports team, but that meant you had free time and the chance to discover a new hobby.

2 Has an opportunity ever come your way that you wanted to say YES to, but felt scared? If you'd said YES to the things that scare you, what would your life be like? Make a list of the opportunities you might have had.

3 Sometimes when we have a dream we really care about, it can feel a bit intense. It's helpful to make time for other things in life that matter to you, besides your dream. Do you have one dream that you are really focused on? If so, what else in life is important to you?

4 Are you facing any big, scary decisions? If so, what are the small steps you can take to help you make your choice? For example, you could think about who might support you with the decision and talk to them about it, you could do some research to help or, if the decision involves doing something new, find a way to give the new thing a try before you decide.

5 When I'm deciding whether or not to say yes to a new opportunity, I ask myself:

WILL I BE HAPPY DOING IT?

IS IT SOMETHING THAT MATTERS TO ME?

DOES IT EXCITE ME?

Do you think these questions could help you to make difficult decisions? If not, what questions can you ask yourself to help you decide what to say yes to?

CHAPTER 3

OUTSIDE OF THE BOX

OUTSIDE OF   THE BOX

With all those big decisions I've had to make in my life, like applying for *Gladiators* and leaving rugby, **it's been really important to stay true to who I am and what I believe in.**

I think that is why I was chosen to be on *Gladiators*.

I brought something different to the table because I was really physical thanks to rugby. I also brought my perspective as a deaf sportswoman. I was honest with the makers of the show about who I am.

THEY CHOSE ME FOR ME.

It was tough, but I was brave enough to step into the unknown with *Gladiators* and, once I was there, I knew I had to keep being brave and show people who Jodie Ounsley really is.

Here are a few of the things that make me, *me*:

1. I'm strong.
2. I'm feminine.
3. I'm competitive.
4. I believe in being kind and caring towards other people.
5. I love being outside, moving, running and jumping.
6. I find joy in the little things in life, like spending time with my family.
7. And . . . I'm scared of cows.

moo

Some people might think that you can't be all of those things at once. Some people might say things like 'You can't be strong *and* feminine', or 'You can't be competitive *and* kind.' But the truth is that every single one of us is unique, and that uniqueness is what makes you, *you*.

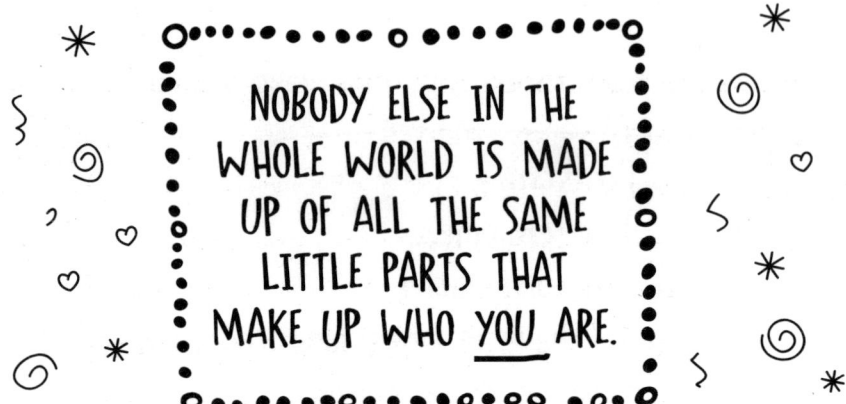

NOBODY ELSE IN THE WHOLE WORLD IS MADE UP OF ALL THE SAME LITTLE PARTS THAT MAKE UP WHO YOU ARE.

Sometimes in life, people will try to put you in a box. As humans, it's easier for our brains if we can organize everyone neatly, so others might try to tell you who you are and how you should act. You might have noticed this in your life already, and if you have, I'm sorry. Although people might not realize that they're doing this, it doesn't feel nice. Trying to fit other people into a box means you aren't appreciating a person for **everything** they are. For example, people might see me smashing into things on TV as Fury and put me in a box labelled 'scary'. But I'm not a scary person. (And they wouldn't think I was scary if they saw me in a field full of cows!)

Boxes are a set shape, and they usually have pretty straight sides, which don't allow for much movement. But I don't like the idea of *anyone* being in a box. That's not how I want to live my life. **I think we should always be pushing at the boundaries of other people's expectations of us.** So how could anyone ever fit inside one small box?

If I'd have just done the things people expected of me, I never would have been on *Gladiators*. People with cochlear implants aren't supposed to play contact sports and if I had accepted that, without trying to find a solution, I would never have started rugby.

On the other hand, once I became an international rugby player, nobody expected me to walk away from that! So, if I'd gone with others' expectations, I definitely would never have left rugby to become a Gladiator.

My mum likes to joke that I wasn't like other kids growing up. I idolized my dad for how strong he was. In our house, strength was always celebrated.

> SOMETIMES GIRLS AREN'T EXPECTED TO BE STRONG, BUT I WAS NEVER TOLD THAT WHEN I WAS GROWING UP.

I really wanted to be able to do what my dad could do. I wanted to be able to lift heavy things, so I'd try to copy his training. We lived in quite a rural area in Yorkshire, and when I was only eight or nine I'd be outside pushing trailers up and down until late at night, copying what my dad did to get stronger.

There was one thing my dad did that I loved more than anything else: coal carrying.

I should probably explain what coal carrying is.

Back in 1963, two men were in a pub in Gawthorpe, Yorkshire, and they decided to have a race to the maypole, which was a pole in the middle of the village. To make things more interesting, they would each do the race carrying a sack of coal on their shoulders.

They wanted to make a proper event of it, so they waited until Easter Monday the following year, when people in the village didn't have to work. They had so much fun that they decided to do it the next year, too. It turned into a yearly event and more and more people started to take part. **Now, more than 400 people sign up each year and there are men's, women's and children's races.** It still takes place every year in a village near where we live, on Easter Monday. It's one of my favourite days of the year.

I remember watching my dad train for the coal-carrying race in the garden when I was younger. He even became world champion in it in 2007, when I was six years old.

I'm too young to remember this, but my dad told me that when I was three years old I picked up a bag of carrots and started sprinting around the kitchen with it on my shoulders, trying to copy him.

You had to be five years old to enter the kids' coal-carrying race, but after that my dad thought it was time to let me take part in the real thing. I was only four at this point, but I was so desperate – my dad didn't tell them my age, so I could join in!

The kids who took part in the race were too small to carry actual sacks of coal on our backs like the adults, so instead we just had a little sack that we carried in our hands.

Even though I was technically too young to enter,
I loved it and I did it every year after that.

I'm telling you about this because the coal-carrying race represents a really key part of who I am. I know it might seem a bit strange. Why would you want to run through a village carrying a sack of coal on your back? But even when I was three years old, my family and I knew what I loved.

I LOVED BEING OUTSIDE, BEING STRONG AND RUNNING FAST. I LOVED COMPETITION, TOO.

I still do. Now, I get the buzz from competition on *Gladiators*, but coal carrying was when I first discovered that feeling. It was my first taste of what it would be like to be an elite athlete. I loved the adrenaline I felt being in a race, with people lining the streets to cheer us on.

> **I WENT ON TO WIN THE WORLD JUNIOR COAL-CARRYING CHAMPIONSHIPS FIVE TIMES.**

For my dad to even enter me into the race in the first place went against what other people expected. I wasn't supposed to be in the race at such a young age and hardly any other girls did it back then. Now, SO many girls take part. The last time I went, they had to put on multiple kids' races because there were so many girls!

Some of them had little blue braids in their hair, like I do when I'm Fury.

It feels amazing. Because I was brave enough to embrace my love of coal carrying, other girls have felt encouraged to embrace it too.

WANTING TO FIT IN CAN FEEL REALLY IMPORTANT AND STRESSFUL.

I struggled with this when I was younger, and even now I still have that feeling sometimes. I had this side of me that loved things like coal carrying, running around and climbing trees. I had always been muscly and strong, and my parents had always made me feel like that was a good thing. Then I discovered rugby and I was rolling around in the mud on weekends. For some people, those weren't the kinds of things girls usually did.

As we got older my friends at school lost interest in sport and became more interested in other things, like fashion. It was tough. **Playing rugby made me feel different from them.** It was a sport that not many girls played and when I tried to start a team at school, the teachers said that girls didn't want to play rugby.

At first, I worried that I needed to change myself to fit in. I wondered if it was normal to want to play such a physical sport when many other girls my age were losing interest in sport altogether. I was really lucky, though – I had an amazing group of friends who supported me, and encouraged me in having different interests from theirs. And when I joined a rugby club, I found another group of girls who loved running into things and getting muddy, just like me. I felt so comfortable around them, and like I didn't need to try to fit into a certain box. **They made me feel like I was just fine as I was.**

It was scary doing something different from my school friends, but I loved rugby and I knew I wanted to give it a go. It turned out to be the right path for me, and it made me realize that **it's so important not to give in to what other people expect of you.**

I think that is the same for a lot of things.

If there's something you like – maybe a subject at school, or a hobby – but other people aren't into it, try to be brave and do it anyway. **If it feels like you're alone, you might not be alone for long.** Others might see what you're doing, think it looks fun and join in.

I know it can feel really scary to be the first person to try something different in your group of friends or in your class. It can be even scarier to try something new when you can't see anyone else who looks like you doing it. **But I promise that if you put yourself out there and do it anyway, it gets so much easier with practice.** And the amazing thing is, you will probably inspire other people to follow your example.

Sometimes, people expect us to behave a certain way. It could be because of how we look or what we're interested in.

BUT WHEN YOU FEEL PASSIONATE ABOUT SOMETHING, OR ARE EVEN JUST INTERESTED IN TRYING SOMETHING NEW, YOU SHOULD GO FOR IT.

Even if it creates an unusual combination.

(Especially if it creates an unusual combination!)

Maybe you love fashion and you also love getting muddy on long hikes. You might want to be a singer and you're also really good at maths.

> # I WANT YOU TO EMBRACE EVERY SINGLE THING THAT MAKES YOU, ## YOU.

When I started doing that, I found life became so much more fun.

Now, rugby is much more popular with girls and I'm so happy about that. But it's still quite common for girls to give up sport at school, especially in secondary school, and I think that's such a shame. **If I'd have tried to fit in by giving up sport, I'd never have started playing rugby for England.** I'd never have got to travel the world playing sport. I wouldn't be on *Gladiators* now.

Of course, sport might not change everyone's life in such an extreme way, but I still think it has so much to offer.

IF YOU DON'T LIKE SPORT, FIND A WAY TO MOVE THAT YOU ENJOY.

When people think of exercise, they often think about going on daily runs, or something like that. It doesn't have to be like that, though. It's just moving your body. Maybe you could give dancing a try, or even just getting outside and going on a walk.

FIND WHAT WORKS FOR YOU.

When you exercise, your body releases chemicals called **endorphins** that make you feel good – if you're having a rubbish day, I promise you'll feel better after a bit of movement.

I've already told you that I'm very caring, but also very competitive.

Both of the 2024 *Gladiators* finalists, Bronte and Marie-Louise, said that I was the toughest Gladiator to compete against. They also said that I was really aggressive during the games, and then really nice backstage.

It might seem strange, but that's just who I am.

I almost scare myself when I go into competitive mode. It's like a rage takes over me.

 **I'M QUITE SHY AS JODIE, BUT AS FURY, I'M FIERCE.**

Sometimes, when we're about to go back into a game, the contenders will try to talk to me. But that doesn't work for me.

I'll have to tell them,

We can't talk right now. I'm ready to go into the game.

I'm not being mean, I'm just in the zone. As soon as the whistle goes on *Gladiators*, I know I'm there to do a job and I'm not going to go easy on the contenders. It doesn't matter how well I get on with them backstage.

It can be confusing for the contenders because, backstage, I'll hug them and tell them they did a really good job. People might expect me to stay in Fury mode and not be kind after the games, but I could never do that. It's not who I am.

In situations like that, when who you are might surprise people, it can make you worry about what people think of you. But you just have to focus on yourself and what makes you happy.

> ## BEING COMPETITIVE MAKES ME HAPPY. BEING KIND TO PEOPLE MAKES ME HAPPY.

So, on *Gladiators*, I do both.

It's also important to surround yourself with people who love you for who you are, not for who they think you should be. **That's why being brave enough to be yourself really matters.** It helps you work out if the people around you are the right people for you. It's natural to feel nervous about fitting in, but no one should make you feel unwelcome because of who you are.

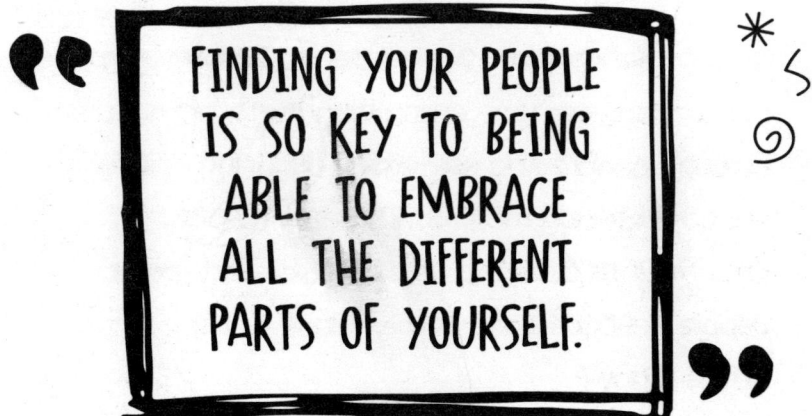

> # FINDING YOUR PEOPLE IS SO KEY TO BEING ABLE TO EMBRACE ALL THE DIFFERENT PARTS OF YOURSELF.

I still worry about what people think sometimes, but I'm not embarrassed about any of the things that make up who I am. I've learned not to let what other people might think change what I'm doing.

DO WHAT FEELS RIGHT FOR YOU.

If I'd listened to what was expected of girls at the age of ten, I'd have stopped running around and climbing trees. Though I didn't know it at the time, *that* was my early preparation to be a Gladiator – so I'm glad I stuck with it!

Later on, when I was a teenager, I could have stopped rugby because none of my friends played it. But I wasn't afraid to do something different, and rugby ended up taking me around the world playing for England. If I'd lived my life in a box built by other people's expectations of me, things would look very different now!

I never want anyone to restrict themselves by allowing other people to put them in a box.

DON'T LET OTHER PEOPLE DEFINE YOU.

You get to decide all of the things that make you, *you*, even if those things are surprising to other people.

I want you to promise yourself that you'll never stop doing something because you're worried about fitting in. Remember that you will find your people, and you'll be happy you stuck with what you love.

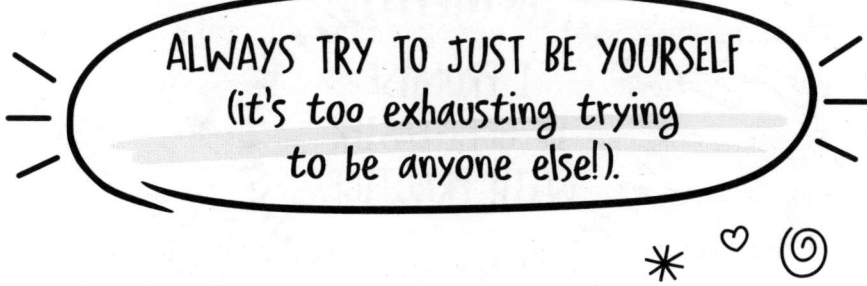

ALWAYS TRY TO JUST BE YOURSELF
(it's too exhausting trying
to be anyone else!).

You can't sum up a person in just one sentence. I don't hide any of the parts that make me, *me,* and that makes me happier.

> ## YOU ARE UNIQUE TOO.

I think that is amazing and I don't want you to hide that. It can be scary to be yourself but **you can tell when someone is being fully, genuinely themselves. They sparkle.**

I want you to get to know all the different parts that make up who you are. Then I want you to embrace them all. That might sound scary now.

I PROMISE
IT GETS EASIER
WITH PRACTICE.

ACTIVITIES

Here are a few more questions to help you think about all the different parts that make up who you are.

I want to help you embrace all those parts. Like in the other chapters, you can write the answers down, draw a spider diagram, talk about them with someone or just have a think in your head.

1 **Close your eyes and take three deep breaths. Now, think about all the different parts that make up who you are. Try not to think of the parts as 'good' or 'bad'. Just list them. It might even be nice to draw a spider diagram for this one. You could put a little stick person in the middle, representing you, then draw lines**

out to all the different parts of yourself. Maybe you're friendly, talkative, funny and shy. Write down any words that come to mind – and know that you can embrace all these different parts of yourself.

2 I loved rugby because I could be completely myself with my teammates. Who are the people you can be completely yourself with? Think about all the people around you: family, friends, teammates or teachers.

3 Ask those people, like a trusted adult or a friend, to give their perspective on all the great things that make you you. You might disagree with them, and that's okay. It can still sometimes be helpful to find out what others see.

4 Have you ever changed what you were doing or how you were behaving because you were worried about what people would think? If so, how did that make you feel? Can you have a think about how your life might be different if you stopped worrying about who other people might expect you to be and, instead, you lived outside the box? If you stopped worrying about what other people think, how would you live your life?

5 What could you do to embrace all the different parts of yourself more? For example, you could write a note to remind you of all the things you love about yourself and read it every morning. You could do some research to find role models who will inspire you, or you could commit to doing one thing that scares you every day!

CHAPTER 4

OVERCOMING BARRIERS

BARRIERS

BREAKTHROUGH

Sometimes it can feel like achieving your dream is impossible, no matter how hard you try to make it happen.

When I found rugby, I thought I'd discovered my path to the Olympics.

I was so excited. But as I watched my brother play from the sidelines, I didn't think I would ever be allowed to join in. To understand why, we need to rewind all the way back to the beginning of my life.

I arrived in the world early: two months before I was supposed to be born. That meant I was quite poorly and had to stay in hospital for the first few months of my life. We don't know for sure, but we think that I became profoundly deaf from some medicine that I was given during that time.

When my parents were told I was deaf, it came as a shock to them. They didn't know anyone else who was deaf, so they didn't really understand what impact it would have on my life. The doctors told them that I would struggle to learn to speak, that I would have a difficult time in school and that it would be hard for me to get a job when I grew up.

They were devastated.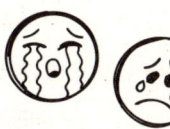

Sometimes in life, you are faced with barriers.

My parents felt like a barrier – bigger than any they could have imagined – had been placed in front of me right at the start of my life. But you've probably gathered by now that Ounsleys don't give up easily! My parents were determined that my life wouldn't be like the one the doctors described. They committed to putting in any work necessary to support me in having a fulfilling life.

One of the big decisions Mum and Dad had to make early on was how to communicate with me. They had the choice of using British Sign Language or trying to support me to learn to speak. There was no right answer in this situation, and both options involved a lot of hard work for everyone. In the end, they decided to try to help me speak.

My parents put in so much effort to help me with that. They did lots of research and found a preschool for deaf children called The Elizabeth Foundation. I started there when I was only three months old. It was a great place for me because everything there was designed for deaf children. They had a music box that children could sit on, so that even if we couldn't hear the music, we could feel the vibrations from the box and experience the music that way.

One really important thing I learned at The Elizabeth Foundation was how to lip-read – which means looking at how people move their lips in order to work out what they are saying. Often, deaf people rely on lip-reading to communicate. I also learned how to pronounce words through lip-reading. Mum and Dad were especially happy that I ended up with a Yorkshire accent like them! People often ask me how this happened, and I'm still not quite sure. My parents have strong Yorkshire accents and I think I did such a good job of copying the way their lips move that I ended up sounding like them.

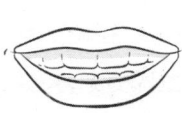 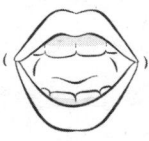 

I don't just rely on lip-reading to communicate, though. When I was only thirteen months old, I had a cochlear implant fitted to help me hear. I was one of the youngest people in the UK at that time to get one! Some deaf people wear hearing aids, which help make sounds around you louder and clearer, but this wasn't an option for me. I have no hearing at all, in either of my ears. That's why I needed a cochlear implant.

This is how my cochlear implant works —

I have a 'processor' on my ear, it's like a little microphone that picks up sound. The 'processor' transmits this sound as electrical impulses to a magnet implanted inside my head. This stimulates a nerve that my brain interprets as sounds, it makes me feel like I can hear things around me. It's very different from a working ear but with a lot of practice I learned to listen and speak.

If you don't understand that, don't worry, I still find it a bit mind-blowing too!

My parents have a video of the moment my implant was turned on for the first time – the very first time that I heard sound. You can see my eyes go really wide, then I just do a little nod like, **'Yep, I hear something!'** It was an amazing moment for my parents.

When I was four, I was able to go to a mainstream school. I had support teachers there, and sometimes, because I couldn't hear everything that was happening in a noisy classroom, they would take me out of class for one-to-one lessons to go through anything I'd missed.

※　◎　＊　ᶜ　♡　＊

Remember the doctors had told my parents I'd struggle to speak and that school would be a challenge too?

WELL, MY PARENTS AND I WORKED HARD AND, MOST IMPORTANTLY, WE BELIEVED WE COULD DO IT. AND WE OVERCAME THOSE BARRIERS TOGETHER.

Because it supported me to hear, the cochlear implant really helped me during that time. But, years later, when it came to rugby, it was a problem. My parents had always been told that having an implant would mean I could never play contact sports. The risk is that if I bumped my head too hard the magnet inside could get dislodged. It isn't always easy to fix a cochlear implant, so there was a chance that, if that happened, I might never be able to hear again.

From the moment they'd found out I was deaf, my parents had always been determined to make sure I had the best life possible. I think I picked up some of my determination from them! That probably explains why, even though I was told my cochlear implant would stop me from playing rugby, I found a way to adapt and play anyway.

At first Mum and Dad told me I just had to accept that I would never be able to play rugby. But you know when someone tells you not to think about something, and then all you can do is think about it? Like, if I tell you not to think about chocolate cake, that's all you can think about now, right? (Sorry if I made you hungry!) It was like that.

ALL THROUGH SCHOOL I HAD NEVER LET BEING DEAF STOP ME FROM DOING ANYTHING.

I worked hard to learn how to lip-read and I put in lots of work to keep up in class when it was difficult to hear. This was the first time my disability had stopped me from doing something I wanted to do.

My parents could see how much I really wanted to play rugby. They could also see that I wouldn't give up. I was relentless, asking them over and over again for months and months if there was anything we could do. Eventually, they got sick of me asking and decided to help me look for a solution.

We started a conversation with the doctors. My dad went back and forth with different specialists to understand the exact risks. We looked into ways that would make playing rugby less dangerous for me. Eventually, we worked out that a scrum cap could help. That's a hat that some rugby players wear to protect their ears while they're playing.

We discovered that we could add extra padding to the scrum cap for more protection. Playing rugby still went against medical advice, but we'd done what we could to make it as safe as possible for me. The doctors told us the risks and in the end the decision to play was up to me and my parents.

Rugby is a contact sport. Whenever anyone plays, they are taking a risk.

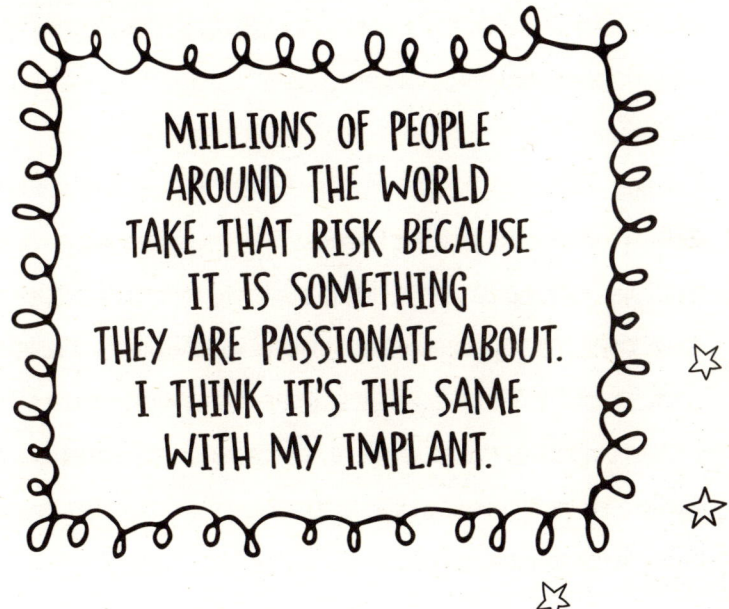

MILLIONS OF PEOPLE AROUND THE WORLD TAKE THAT RISK BECAUSE IT IS SOMETHING THEY ARE PASSIONATE ABOUT. I THINK IT'S THE SAME WITH MY IMPLANT.

> I DON'T WANT TO HOLD BACK AND LIVE WITH REGRETS. AND I ESPECIALLY DON'T WANT MY HEARING TO HOLD ME BACK.

It would have been easy for my mum and dad to stand their ground when they were worried, because they love me and they don't want anything bad to happen to me. They were amazing for being open to changing their opinion and supporting me in finding ways around the problem.

I never wanted to ignore or disrespect the doctors. I didn't want to be reckless with my cochlear implant either. I wanted to work *with* the doctors, and they recognized that. Instead of just accepting that I couldn't do something and walking away, I started an honest and respectful conversation, which meant we could work together to find a way around the problem.

I know that it is always *my* responsibility to wear head protection when I'm playing. I had to wear my scrum cap every single time I played, even during training sessions. If I ever forgot it, I wouldn't play.

Now when I go for my regular check-ups with the doctors they tell me they've loved following my journey in rugby and on *Gladiators*.

I HOPE THAT THE BARRIERS YOU FACE IN YOUR LIFE AREN'T AS EXTREME AND DANGEROUS AS THE ONE I FACED IN RUGBY.

The doctors were saying no for a very good reason, but that doesn't mean I had to accept what they were saying without exploring whether there were any solutions. If my parents had kept saying no too, I would have had to admit that maybe rugby wasn't a very good idea. Their support reassured me that it was worth *trying*, though.

If you find you are facing a barrier in life, talk to people about it. Find support from

the people around you to help you find a solution. Remember that you don't have to just accept barriers. Look at your options and see if there are any ways to get around problems, or at least make the problems a bit smaller. For example, if you're struggling at maths, you *could* just accept that maths just isn't one of your strengths. But if you

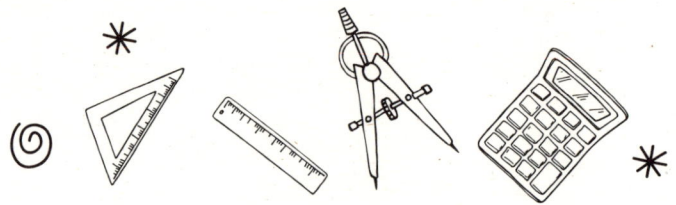

want to get better at it, think about what you have around you that could help.

Is there someone you know who's good at maths who could help you?

Are there any books you could look at or extra worksheets you could do to learn more?

YOU CAN GET A LONG WAY BY WORKING HARD AND BEING DETERMINED.

It's a bit like one of those mazes you sometimes get in magazines or puzzle books. You start out drawing a route, then you might come up against a dead end. So you go backwards on yourself and try another route. Eventually, possibly after lots of different scribbles on the page, you find the right path that gets you to where you want to be.

Of course, sometimes there are barriers that we just can't get around, even if we try really, really hard. Having to leave my Olympic dream behind was one of those situations for me. Some barriers force us to change our direction and come up with a new plan. It might seem really tough in the moment when you haven't been able to get what you want, but I have found in my life that those changes of direction sometimes lead to the most exciting things. After all, that's how I ended up on *Gladiators*!

Being deaf has made me really good at adapting to different situations to get around any barriers. It has opened my eyes to the fact that sometimes I have to find a solution that will make a difficult situation a bit easier. When someone says no to you, unless you see that it is for an important reason, don't see it as something that is already decided. See it as a chance to try to find a solution. It might not be a quick fix. It might take time. If you've tried and it turns out to be a barrier you can't overcome, be open to the new direction that it sends you in.

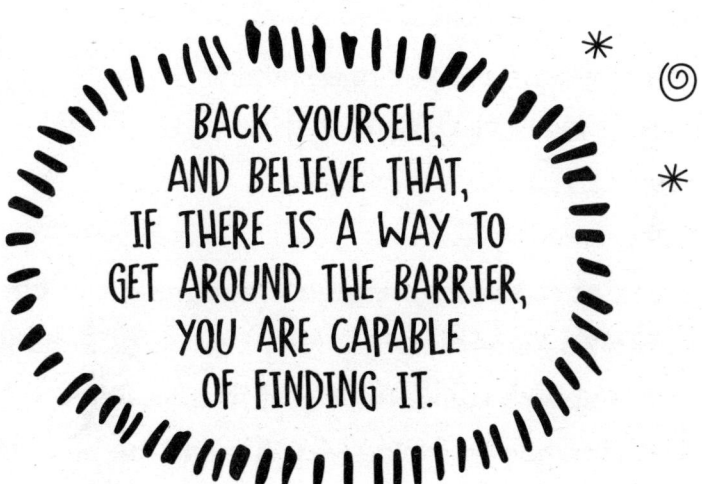

BACK YOURSELF,
AND BELIEVE THAT,
IF THERE IS A WAY TO
GET AROUND THE BARRIER,
YOU ARE CAPABLE
OF FINDING IT.

ACTIVITIES

If there are barriers between you and your dreams, here are a few questions to get you thinking about ways around them.

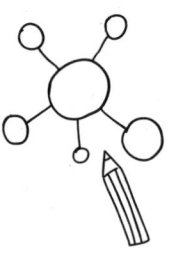

You can write your answers down, talk them through with someone, draw a spider diagram or just have a think in your head. Find the way that works best for you.

1 **Think about something you really want in life. It could be something you want to do at school — join a sports team, take part in a musical performance or a play — or it might be something you want to do when you're older. Do you think there are any barriers that are in the way of you achieving your dream?**

2 If you are facing a barrier to something you want, what are your options to get around it? Try to think of every possible option you can. Even if you think you've thought of everything, ask yourself: are there any more options? The more options you have to choose from, the more chance you have of getting around barriers.

3 Who could offer you support and help to get around barriers in your life? What trusted adults, family or friends could you turn to? How will you ask for their support?

4 Have you ever faced a barrier that you couldn't overcome? How did that feel? Did you have to move in a different direction because of the barrier? Did any good things come from that?

5 Can you think of a time when a situation
seemed impossible but you eventually found a
solution? Think about what happened, where
you were and who was involved. What did you
learn from that situation that you could use
again in the future?

CHAPTER 5

OUR DIFFERENCES ARE OUR SUPERPOWERS

OUR

DIFFERENCES ARE

OUR

SUPERPOWERS

THERE'S NO SUCH THING AS NORMAL.

It took me a while to get my head around that. But once I accepted it to be true, my life changed.

For as long as I can remember, I knew
I was different from my friends –
I had a cochlear implant, and other
people didn't. I used to tell people it
was my 'robot ear'.

At around the age of ten, I started to notice that I was struggling in lessons, and no one else around me seemed to be struggling. I couldn't always hear what the teachers were saying so it was harder for me to learn in a classroom. On top of that, I was really shy. I didn't have the confidence to tell the teachers that I was missing things. I was worried that it would make me a burden on people. I even used to hide my cochlear implant under my hair because I didn't want anyone else to see it.

Growing up, I always thought being different was bad. I didn't want to stand out; I just wanted to fit in.

Later in my life, the stress of not feeling 'normal' – feeling different from everyone around me – almost made me give up the thing I loved. When I was sixteen, I left home and went to college in Loughborough, about two hours away from my house, because they had a really good rugby team there. It was a brilliant opportunity to get better at the sport, and overall it was a great experience. But while I was there, I considered giving up rugby altogether.

Just like in the classroom at school, communication was always a challenge for me in rugby. It's a team sport and you need to be able to understand what your teammates want so that you can all work together. Being a deaf person in a team of hearing people took a lot of hard work. Rugby is played on a big pitch and coaches and teammates have to shout loudly to each other to communicate and be able to play together as a team. Shouting across the pitch doesn't work for me, because I need to look at people's faces and lip-read to understand them. But I didn't have the confidence to speak up and ask for what I needed. **Now, it seems so obvious to me that I should tell people when I'm struggling so they can support me.** But back then, I was so shy and I just felt like I couldn't ask for help because I was the one who wasn't 'normal'.

**I didn't want to stand out.
So I kept quiet.**

I got my first big injury when I was at college. I was training with the England Under-18 team, practising tackles, when I dislocated my shoulder. That meant I missed out on six months of training with my team at Loughborough, and it really knocked my confidence. I was worried about whether I would still play well when I eventually returned to training. When my worries about my injury were added to the challenges I already had because I couldn't hear my teammates, it felt really hard. I felt like I didn't know people well enough to tell them that I was struggling, so I kept it to myself.

Remember I said I always want you to back yourself and believe in yourself? Well, I know that's not always easy. Sometimes it can just feel too hard. That's how I felt at Loughborough. My injury meant I couldn't play rugby for a long time, so when I finally did return, I thought

I wasn't good enough at the sport any more. I was back in training with my team and struggling to hear. It felt like there were too many challenges. I wasn't sure I was enjoying it any more, either. It was so frustrating because rugby was something I really wanted to do and was passionate about, but I felt like the thing that made me different, my deafness, was making it difficult.

Sometimes it feels like people forget that I'm deaf. To understand what someone is saying, I have to put together the sound that I get from my cochlear implant and the way they are moving their lips, then I have to guess to fill any gaps that are left. It's hard work. I'm really good at it so I think sometimes people don't realize that it takes a lot of concentration and effort for me to communicate. **I'm also a really positive person. At Loughborough, even though I was struggling, I was smiling and trying to**

get on with things. I didn't want to tell my teammates or coaches how difficult things were.

Eventually, I opened up to my mum. I told her I was having a tough time and that I didn't feel good enough. That it was even making me think rugby wasn't for me any more. She has a friend who is a psychologist, so she suggested that I talk to them.

Talking to a psychologist can seem like a big deal, but Mum thought it might help me find my confidence again. And she was right. I found it so powerful to talk to someone about what was worrying me. I'd had all of these thoughts swirling around my head: worrying about not hearing, what my teammates were saying, whether I was good enough for the team.

I talked to the psychologist about why I wasn't feeling confident and why I thought I couldn't talk to my teammates about being deaf. We discussed what I enjoyed about rugby, and reminding myself that I just love running around and smashing into people helped me to love the sport again. From talking things through and understanding what was causing some of my worries, I started to change the way I was thinking. **I started to approach things more positively, instead of worrying about what might go wrong all the time.** That kind of change can be scary and take a long time, so I still didn't always feel confident enough to talk to my teammates about being deaf, but my confidence in rugby and love of the game returned.

As my confidence grew and I remembered to enjoy my time on the rugby pitch, I became a stronger player. When I was eighteen, I moved to London to join the England Sevens team. That's when things changed for me. It was my first experience on a professional team, and I soon learned that in order for my team and me to be able to work together, I couldn't hide my deafness. I couldn't pretend that everything was fine. If I didn't hear something in a training session, I wouldn't know what we were supposed to be doing and it would have an impact on the team as a whole.

The lightbulb moment for me came when everyone in the team had to do a presentation to tell our teammates about ourselves. I was terrified to stand up in front of new people and all of the England coaches, but I didn't want to carry on trying to pretend I was the same as everyone else, like I had done at Loughborough. So, I took the opportunity to tell the team what it's like to live as a deaf person.

That was a huge moment for me. It was pretty scary, but as soon as I did it my teammates and coaches were so willing to learn how to adapt things to make it easier for me.

I told my teammates that I couldn't hear what they were saying if they were far away — instead, I asked them to come over to talk to me when we were on the pitch.

When the coaches were introducing new tactics, I would ask them to tell me directly rather than shouting it across the field to everyone.

On top of that, I had extra meetings with the coaches to go over things I might have missed in training sessions.

I'd thought that telling people about being deaf would cause problems. I'd thought people would think I was being difficult. But the opposite happened. Once I embraced my deafness, it was clear that people were willing and happy to adapt to help me.

> " I REALIZED THAT WHEN YOU TELL PEOPLE WHAT YOU NEED, USUALLY THEY WANT TO SUPPORT YOU. IT WAS A HUGE WEIGHT LIFTED OFF MY SHOULDERS. "

Once I'd been honest about how being deaf affected me in rugby, I started to feel more confident talking about it in other areas too. I had always had a black processor on my cochlear implant because I thought a dark colour would help me hide it under my hair. As I got older, I'd started to see other people wearing white processors, and I thought they looked so bold.

It stood out *so* much. I started asking myself,

Why is standing out a bad thing?

Talking about my deafness helped me to feel proud about wearing a cochlear implant. So, when I was twenty-one, I got a white processor. Now I prefer it to my black one.

It took me a long time to learn how to embrace the things that make me different. It's natural to feel like you want to fit in with the people around you, especially when you're growing up.

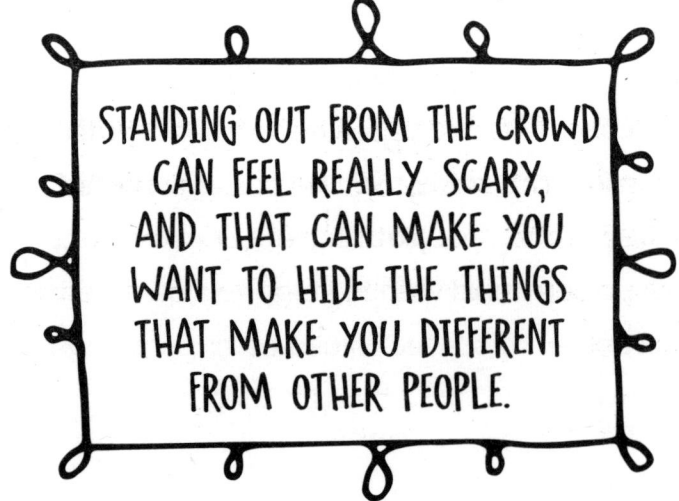

STANDING OUT FROM THE CROWD CAN FEEL REALLY SCARY, AND THAT CAN MAKE YOU WANT TO HIDE THE THINGS THAT MAKE YOU DIFFERENT FROM OTHER PEOPLE.

But even with your closest friends, there will be lots of things that make you different from each other.

OUR DIFFERENCES ARE WHAT MAKE US **UNIQUE.** THEY'RE OUR SUPERPOWERS.

Embracing the things that make you different can bring so much confidence and happiness to your life. It can be so draining if you're constantly trying to hide a part of yourself.

Embracing what makes you different can help people around you to support you, too.

Maybe you've had a tough situation with your friends or teachers at school. You might be having a hard time and nobody knows because you're doing your best to act like everything is okay. I learned a huge lesson at Loughborough: you have to tell people what you need if you want them to support you. People aren't mind readers; often they won't know you're struggling unless you tell them you are. Rather than bottling it all up, it can help even just to say something as small as, 'I am not feeling totally myself today'. That will help people to understand.

IT'S OKAY TO ASK FOR WHAT YOU NEED.

By the time I joined *Gladiators*, I was confident talking about my deafness and had started using my social media to tell people about my life as a deaf person. Because of that, the makers of *Gladiators* knew I would need some things on the programme to be adapted for me. Before I joined the show, everyone working on it had training to learn about how to support deaf people, so that I would feel more comfortable. I was so shocked and thought that was amazing. We had conversations about what I would need: we looked at how my helmet would work with my implant, and now the referee does arm signals as well as using a whistle to stop and start the games, so I don't have to rely on hearing the whistle.

There are lots of little things like that to help me do my job as Fury. I know now that asking for adjustments like that isn't a burden on people. It's just what I need because I'm deaf. Now, I think:

I've got a disability, what's bad about that?

Of course, being deaf comes with lots of challenges, but I also think it's a bit like a superpower.

I SEE THINGS DIFFERENTLY FROM OTHER PEOPLE BECAUSE I AM DIFFERENT FROM OTHER PEOPLE.

I love that about myself. If I wasn't deaf, I'd be a completely different person.

Here are a few of the things being deaf has taught me:

✳ Being deaf can mean a lot of barriers in life, so I am great at adapting to challenges.

✳ Because of the challenges I have faced, I AM BRAVE.

✳ In situations when it is hard for me to hear, like on trains or other places where there is background noise, I often have to rely on other people to help me, so I am an open and chatty person.

✳ I know what it feels like to struggle, so I know when other people are having a hard time and I try to be a good person and support them.

This is why describing things as 'normal' isn't helpful. Instead of encouraging people to celebrate their differences, it makes people who aren't considered 'normal' feel bad. It's an especially unhelpful word for disabled people. For example, people might say I haven't got 'normal hearing', but that puts a negative spin on my disability. It suggests that being a hearing person is the right way to be. Being hearing isn't 'normal' – it's just different from being deaf.

On *Gladiators*, I want to change people's perceptions of what 'normal' looks like.

WHAT ACTUALLY IS 'NORMAL' ANYWAY?

IT'S JUST AN IMAGE WE HAVE BUILT OUT OF NOWHERE.

I am so proud to be a deaf Gladiator. The way people have responded to me being on the show has been amazing; it's more than I could ever have imagined. Because I embrace my cochlear implant and am honest about my disability, I see kids in schools now who have multi-coloured hearing aids or implants. I'm so happy that they're embracing their deafness, too.

ONE OF THE BEST THINGS THAT I'VE LEARNED THROUGH ALL THIS IS THAT DIFFERENCES MAKE A TEAM STRONGER.

If every player on a rugby team was exactly the same shape and size, with the same skills, you wouldn't have a very good team.

You need wingers who are quick and can finish off tries. You need your forwards to be powerful and strong. You need play-makers who work out the best tactics to beat your opposition. **Everyone's different strengths combine to make the team stronger.**

Often, we can't help comparing ourselves to other people, and thinking about whether we are better or worse than them.

> I STILL COMPARE MYSELF TO OTHER PEOPLE, BUT WHEN I NOTICE I'M DOING IT, I TRY TO THINK INSTEAD ABOUT ALL THE THINGS THAT MAKE ME DIFFERENT FROM OTHERS.

And then I remind myself to celebrate those things. I actually think a world where everyone is the same as each other would be really boring. We'd all have the same personality and do the same things.

Where's the fun in that?

ACTIVITIES

Hopefully you know the drill by now. Have a think about these questions, write them down, talk to someone about them or draw yourself a fancy spider diagram.

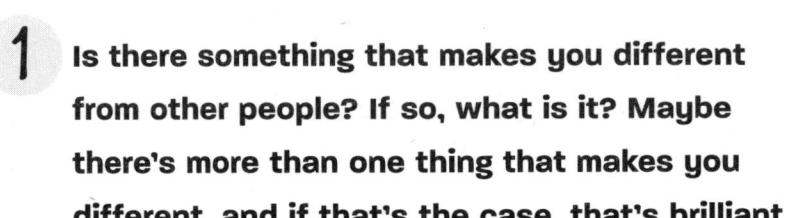

1 Is there something that makes you different from other people? If so, what is it? Maybe there's more than one thing that makes you different, and if that's the case, that's brilliant.

2 How do you feel about the things that make you different? Have you been hiding them from other people, like I tried to hide my deafness? After reading this chapter, how do you feel about the things that make you different?

3 Once I was honest about the challenges that being deaf brought to my life, people around me could support me. Is there anything you need support with that you are keeping to yourself? How could you share it with people?

4 Think about some people you know who are different from you. How could you celebrate their differences? Is there anything you can do to support them?

5 Being deaf has made me braver, more adaptable and better at connecting with people. What strengths do your differences bring you? How have your differences changed your life for the better?

CHAPTER 6

TEAMWORK MAKES THE DREAM WORK

TEAM

WORK

MAKES THE

DREAM

WORK

I couldn't have done any of the things I've talked about in this book without support. Chasing my dreams, changing my dreams and embracing my differences – all of those things would have been *so* difficult without an amazing team of people around me.

I'VE BEEN LUCKY IN MY LIFE BECAUSE I'VE BEEN PART OF SOME GREAT TEAMS.

My family is one of those teams: Mum and Dad have been an amazing support for me. My friends are another: I had a brilliant group at school who got me through tiring days of learning with lots of laughter. I had great rugby teammates and, of course, now I'm part of the *Gladiators* team.

I've worked hard to get to where I am in my life, but I know I couldn't have done it on my own. **We all need good people around us to help us keep going.**

Being part of a professional sports team showed me that it is easier to achieve your dreams if you work together. When you've got a really big goal in your sights, like the Olympics, the work you have to put in to get there can be tough. When you're doing it with other people, all training hard for the same thing, **it feels so good to know that you're all in it together.** In the darker moments, when things feel really hard, you have people to lean on.

My parents have been there for me in some really tough moments. And they've also inspired me with the way they've lived their lives.

I get my personality from my mum. She's hardworking, kind and caring. She likes bringing people together and she makes me want to be a good person, like her. That's why I enjoy being on TV and getting to meet lots of people, because it has helped me do some good in the world.

When it comes to being a sportsperson, I've got that from my dad. As well as being a World Coal-Carrying Champion and a *Gladiators* contender, he was a mixed martial arts professional. He never pushed me to be a sportsperson, though, I just loved sport because he was doing it. Remember I said he was on *Gladiators* when I was only seven? When he was on the show as a contender, he set up all the different events at home so I could practise them with him. We had rings in the barn for Hang Tough, he made a climbing wall in the garage, and he put a ladder on the ceiling and attached a rope to it for me to swing across. When I actually got to be on *Gladiators*, he helped me prepare for that, too. 'The Edge' was the event I was most nervous about, so Dad got some old planks and put them on the grass for me to practise running in a zig-zag, like we do on the show.

My parents have shown me what good support looks like, so now I do my best to offer the same to other people. I always try to be a good teammate, and the most important part of that for me is trust.

I WANT PEOPLE TO BE ABLE TO TALK TO ME AND KNOW THAT THEY CAN TRUST ME WITH WHAT THEY SHARE.

It's really important to have people around you that you can trust. I've needed that because my life has started to be filled with so many amazing opportunities, but being so busy also comes with challenges.

I started to have so many exciting invitations coming in from all over the country and it felt like I was always going to such cool events – I even went to Buckingham Palace once! It was amazing.

But when things change in your life it's so important to have people around you who can keep you grounded and who you can be yourself around. My friends, family and rugby teammates have all done that for me.

My life as a professional sportsperson started getting busier and busier. When I get asked to do things that sound interesting – like a radio or TV interview, or an event that's far away from home – I always want to say yes because it all seems so exciting and I don't like to let people down.

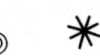

Being a kind person is really important to me, so if someone asks me for help with an event, I always want to do it. However, that means that even if I'm really tired, I sometimes pretend I'm fine and I say yes.

But I started to get so busy that I began to feel drained. I was always travelling or at events and I didn't have any time to relax and do the things I would usually do to recharge. I got more and more tired until I just didn't feel like myself any more. Normally, this is something I'd talk to my parents about, but I didn't want to tell them how I was feeling because I didn't want to seem ungrateful about all the opportunities I was getting.

Eventually, it became too much. There was one morning when I felt so overwhelmed that I started crying and I didn't really understand why. I'd had four days in a row of travelling all over the country for events. I was feeling so tired, and I had started to get ill. **I knew it was time to be honest with my team.** I told my mum that I felt like I was working too much, and she was so supportive.

She told me she wished I'd said something sooner so that she could've helped me. We sat down together and made a plan to move things around so that I could have more rest. She helped me to feel like myself again. My mum just wants me to be happy, and she always wants to be there for me if I'm not feeling great. She helped me to see that if you don't ask the people around you for help or lean on them when things are tough, you end up holding everything in yourself. And that's a lot of pressure on your shoulders.

It's extra important for me that I'm honest about my energy levels because of something called hearing fatigue. When I was younger, I used to get really bad migraines (headaches that would make me feel really sick). I got them constantly and we couldn't figure out what was causing them. We thought it might be because I needed glasses, but when I got some they didn't make a difference. Eventually, I learned about hearing fatigue.

Because it takes so much concentration for me to lip-read and fill in gaps that I've missed in conversation, my brain becomes overworked and really, really tired. I think that's what caused my migraines.

Now, I've learned to listen to my
body and look for signs of hearing
fatigue before it's too late and I start
to feel ill. As soon as I feel
that my energy levels are
starting to drop and I am
struggling to concentrate
on what people are saying,
I know it's time to take a break.

I know more now about what causes hearing
fatigue, and that helps me to manage it. I've been
invited to events where I meet lots of new people
and there is a lot of background noise, like music.
Those sorts of situations are challenging because
it's hard to hear people with all the noise and
it's difficult to lip-read with people I've never met
before, because I have to learn their lip patterns
to be able to do it. I know that being in an
environment like that for a couple of hours makes

me feel like I'm fizzling out. I have to manage my energy levels and take breaks, stepping outside when I need to.

Sometimes, I just have to say no to things. I still find this quite hard, because I always want to help people, but my friends and my family often support me to understand when I need to slow down. Because my mum is kind and caring like me, she knows that when you want to help everyone all the time, sometimes you forget to look after yourself. She reminds me to take breaks and put myself first when I need to.

I used to believe that saying no when people asked me for help would make them instantly dislike me and think I was being disrespectful. But now I know that's just not true.

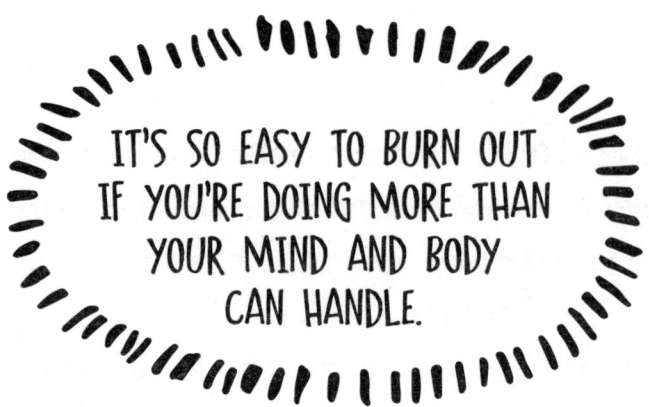

IT'S SO EASY TO BURN OUT IF YOU'RE DOING MORE THAN YOUR MIND AND BODY CAN HANDLE.

Playing sevens for England taught me that you can't be in 'game mode' all the time; you have to take breaks and look after yourself. At sevens tournaments, you have to play a lot of short, 14-minute matches over the course of three days. You play on a full-sized rugby pitch, and that is a lot of space to cover when you only have seven people on your team, so you have to run really far and really fast. It would be impossible to go at full-speed, non-stop, for three days. Who would have the energy for that? When I was playing sevens I had to learn to switch on for 14 minutes while I played the match, then switch off and rest immediately after so that I was ready to go for the next one.

For me to be able to contribute to the team as a good teammate, taking time to rest properly was just as important as all the running around. It's the same now. Helping people means so much to me, but I know I can't say yes every single time someone asks, because I have to switch off sometimes so that I can be at my best when I am able to help.

With hearing fatigue, it's especially important to give myself time to recharge, and I am always my most relaxed when I have my team around me. I travel all over the country working, but my home is still in Yorkshire with my parents, because that's where I'm comfortable and feel most like myself. When I'm recharging, I want to be with the people I love. My happy place is wherever I'm with the people I love most — especially if there's good food there too!

Sometimes it helps to take off the processor of my cochlear implant and have a bit of quiet for a while. When I have hearing fatigue, sound can feel so overwhelming and exhausting. If I take my processor off, I can't hear anything and I feel like I'm in my own little world. I completely shut off from everything around me and it feels like I'm resetting my brain. When I know I have a few days in a row of going to different events, I plan a day off where I can shut down and catch up on sleep to get my energy back.

> # IT IS SO MUCH EASIER TO BE WHO YOU ARE, AND ACHIEVE YOUR DREAMS, WHEN YOU HAVE THE RIGHT SUPPORT.

It's so important that you surround yourself with a team of people who can rally round you. It might be your parents, aunties or uncles, or it could be friends or teammates, if you play sport.

You know you've found the right team when you find people you can be completely yourself around. You feel warm and relaxed when you're with them. You don't feel on edge, and you don't feel like you have to behave a certain way to fit in.

> ## YOUR BEST SUPPORTERS ARE THOSE WHO ACCEPT YOU FOR WHO YOU ARE.

Once you've found your crew, be honest with them. Having a good team means being surrounded by people who want the best for you and want to support you. If you're struggling with something, you're not causing a problem by talking to somebody about it. **Bottling up your problems and pretending everything is fine doesn't help.** You just end up tiring yourself out and feeling rubbish. I know it can feel scary to share how you're really feeling with others. And there are loads of things, big and small, that you might be worried about. You might be feeling overwhelmed about some schoolwork you have to do, nervous about a sports game you have coming up, or you might feel upset by something a friend said to you. If you're scared to speak up, try to think about why you don't want to share your problem. Is it because you're embarrassed about what people will think? Is it because you think they won't be understanding? Sometimes you might believe your problem is too small to bother your team with, but if you're struggling with something, however big or small it is, your team will want to know. When I have doubts like that, I remind myself how my family and friends have supported me in the past and I know I don't need to worry about sharing my problems.

You don't have to make a big announcement. You can just say something small so people know that you're not feeling totally yourself, or that something is bothering you. Have the confidence to speak up about things, because sharing your problems is actually one way that you can find your best supporters. And if you're honest with the people who support you, they'll be honest back.

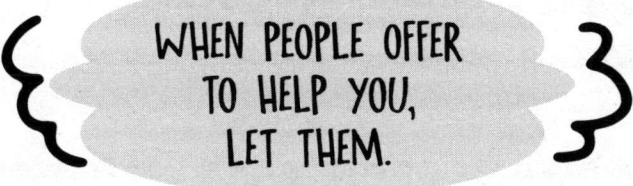

WHEN PEOPLE OFFER TO HELP YOU, LET THEM.

If you're having a hard time and someone comes to your aid, you know they're someone you can rely on in the future. And remember, being part of a team isn't just about getting support — it's about offering support to your teammates in return, too. *

ACTIVITIES

Here are some questions to get you thinking more about the advice in this chapter, so you can always be sure you have the best people around you, supporting you.

1 Think about the different people you know and how you feel after you've spent time with them. Who can you be totally yourself with? Who makes you feel relaxed? Who are your best supporters?

2 Have you ever felt completely exhausted, like I did? What had you been doing? What signs could you look out for to stop yourself getting exhausted in the future?

3 Close your eyes, take three deep breaths, then think about your happy place. Where are you? What are you doing? For example, you might be outside in nature, watching TV or reading.

4 Are you with other people or on your own? Think about all the details that make up your happy place — and remember them so that next time you need to recharge, you know where you need to be, what you need to be doing and who you need to be with.

5 It's important to be honest with your team, so that they can support you. Can you think of a time when you've shared a problem with someone? How did it feel afterwards? Who supported you?

6 A good teammate supports other people on their team. Who do you want to support? What can you do to support them in return?

CHAPTER 7

SPEAK UP

SPEAK

UP

Since I was young, I've had a fire inside me; I knew I wanted to help people and make a difference in the world. But when I was younger, I didn't know exactly how I could do this or what difference I would be able to make.

When I was at college, I wanted to explore this fire more and try to understand what I could do to help people. I was chasing my dream to get to the Olympics, but I wanted to do something alongside that to have an impact on people's lives.

I had some amazing role models growing up, who made such a difference for me, and I wondered if I could be that person for someone else. My role models helped me work out how I wanted to live my life. It was eight-time gold medallist Usain Bolt who helped me to see that my dream was to go to the Olympics. Jessica Ennis-Hill was an Olympian I could relate to even more, because she is a woman and she represented Great Britain, like I wanted to. Seeing people achieving the things you're dreaming of can be so powerful in helping you to believe that you can achieve those things too.

My parents have been great role models as well: my dad inspired me to be an athlete, and my mum showed me how to be a good person.

Then there was my Auntie Jane. Auntie Jane and I were really close. She lost her eyesight when she was sixteen and she showed me that as disabled people we don't have to just accept what society expects of us. Society isn't designed for disabled people, and that can make it harder for me to do the things I want to do, but Auntie Jane tried not to let being blind stop her from doing exactly what she wanted. She showed me how important it is to adapt in order to get around barriers; she inspired me to not let anything get in my way in having the life that I want for myself.

We often used to walk to the corner shop together to get sweets. Normally her partner, who wasn't blind, would come with us to guide Auntie Jane. But there was one day when he was working, so I assumed that meant we couldn't go. We had to cross a busy road to get to the shop – I thought it would be too dangerous because Auntie Jane couldn't see the cars and I couldn't hear them. But she didn't accept that. She told me,

So I told her if I could see any cars coming and she told me if she could hear any. We worked together, and we got safely across the road and got our sweets. It might seem like a small thing, but it felt really scary to try to cross the road when I couldn't hear and Auntie Jane couldn't see. It was such an important lesson for me; it was when I learned not to let my disability hold me back.

Auntie Jane and all the other role models I had growing up had an incredible impact on my life. But I never had a deaf role model. And I didn't know anyone deaf who wanted to be a sportsperson, like I did. I was England's first deaf female rugby player and I'm the first deaf UK Gladiator, but I don't want to be the *only* deaf person to ever do these things. That's what being a role model means to me: showing others what is possible so they can do it too.

After I joined England Sevens, I started to understand how I could become a role model to deaf children. As I was just eighteen at the time, I was given a mentor.

A mentor is a bit like a role model; it's someone you talk to regularly who gives you advice to help you work out what you want to do and how you can start doing it.

My mentor had a great idea to help me get started — she suggested that I could start visiting deaf schools to tell pupils about my rugby career. Speaking in front of a room full of kids felt scary, but the idea of working with other deaf people made that fire inside me burn even brighter. It felt right.

I did my research and made a list of all the deaf schools in England, then I started sending out emails.

I told the schools my story and asked if I could come in and do an assembly to tell people about myself. There were nine schools and they all said yes. So when I wasn't playing rugby, I started travelling around the country to meet their pupils.

IT WAS AMAZING.

I saw the impact my story could have on these kids. When I saw someone celebrating their cochlear implant because they saw me being proud to wear mine, it lifted my mood to another level. I felt so warm and happy when I was speaking to the kids. I felt like it was exactly what I was supposed to be doing.

I HAD FOUND MY CAUSE.

Back then, I had to invite myself into the schools because nobody knew who I was or that I was trying to play rugby for England. That was five years ago. Now that I'm on *Gladiators* and more people know me, schools invite me in to do talks. I'm doing the same thing I've always done, just on a way bigger scale. Now, though, I focus on trying to speak to all disabled kids and not just the deaf community.

When I was a baby, my parents were given such negative messages about how my life would turn out. Remember they were told I wouldn't speak, go to school or get a job? Well, **we smashed those barriers** and now it's really important to me that I speak up and show disabled people that, even if the world doesn't think you can achieve something, *you* get to define who you are and what you're capable of.

> **YOU CAN OVERCOME BARRIERS.**

> ## IF YOU BACK YOURSELF AND BELIEVE IN YOURSELF, YOU CAN DO THE THING THAT MAKES YOU HAPPY.

It turns out that message has helped kids who aren't disabled, too, and I love that. No matter who you are, no matter your background, everyone faces challenges in their lives. And everyone has to find a way to work around those barriers. So if I can help kids, even in some small way, figure out how to do that, I'm happy.

Parents often tell me that I'm a sporting role model for their daughters – just like Jessica Ennis-Hill was for me – and that feels amazing. They send me pictures of their girls trying rugby for the first time with blue braids in their hair, like I have on *Gladiators*, and they tell me they're embracing their Fury on the pitch. **It's so heartwarming** — just one message like that can make my whole day better. I feel so lucky that I have a platform that I can use to inspire people in this way. Every time I speak up and share my message I think,

I ABSOLUTELY LOVE THIS.

Over time I discovered other ways I could make a difference, besides the school visits. I've worked with England Football, supporting the work they do to

make football more accessible for disabled children, and I speak to doctors about my experience so they can help the families of other profoundly deaf people.

One thing that's really important to me is raising awareness of what it's like to live as a deaf person. I use social media for this. I want people to understand that, most of the time, I feel like I'm a deaf person in a world that's designed for hearing people. It feels like the world was made a certain way, and I have to work hard to fit into that. **It can be exhausting.**

A good example is when I'm travelling by train. I went on my first train when I was twenty-three years old, because before that I didn't feel confident enough to use them. I have to put in a lot of work to travel by train; I have my cochlear implant, but with all the background noise in a train station, that's not enough to help me hear an announcement. That can make it hard to find the platform for my train, and it's even more difficult if there are late changes that are only announced over the loudspeaker. Once I'm on the train, I can't hear all of the stops when they're announced either, so that means that I have to be on high alert and I always have to plan ahead. I have to look online to find the information I need, or I might have to speak to other passengers and ask them for help. Thankfully, there's a bit more awareness about deafness now, which means there are more visual things to help me – like stops displayed on screens inside the train carriages. But it can still feel isolating when you're constantly trying to fit into a system that wasn't designed for you.

I think it's really important that I tell people about challenges like that, so we can call for changes to be made that work for deaf people. A few years ago I started seeing disability awareness videos on social media, and I thought they were a great way to teach people about different disabilities.

IT'S IMPORTANT TO TALK ABOUT OUR DIFFERENCES AND NOT JUST PRETEND THAT EVERYONE IN THE WORLD IS THE SAME.

So I decided to do a video where I took off the processor of my cochlear implant and explained a bit about how it works. I was quite nervous about posting it, but I was so happy with how people reacted to it. People had so many questions and I was glad to be able to talk to them about something that is so important in my life. I got such a positive reaction that I've kept doing those videos, focusing particularly on some of the challenges of being deaf, like hearing fatigue.

You remember that fire inside me that I spoke about at the beginning of the chapter? I want you to try to find your very own version of that inside you.

I know now that helping people understand disabilities and inspiring others to try to overcome the barriers in their lives are what keeps the fire lit inside me. But that doesn't mean those have to be your things too. I want you to find something you really believe in and care about, because

WHEN YOU SPEAK UP ABOUT A CAUSE AND WORK TO MAKE A DIFFERENCE, IT FEELS AMAZING.

You might not know yet what lights the fire inside you, and that is totally okay. I wasn't sure either at first. If there's something you think you might be a bit interested in, **give it a go**. You can always speak to other people who are already working to make a change in this area to find out more about it. It might spark something, or you might realize you're actually not as interested as you thought you were and move on to something else. If you're unsure about what you might want to do, you could have a look at ways you can volunteer in your community – for example, there might be a sports club or local community centre that needs some help, or something you can do to support people younger than you in your school.

It could be good to think about what feels unfair to you in this world. For me, it doesn't seem fair that the world isn't designed for disabled people and that we're often at a disadvantage because of that. There might be something you really care about because of an experience you or someone you love has had.

Some people want to protect the environment, others really care about animals, or it might be something in your school that you've always thought would work better in a different way.

If there's something in this world that you want to change, you *can* do something about it. You don't have to just accept it.

YOU ARE POWERFUL AND YOU CAN CREATE CHANGE.

Even really small actions can add up to make a big difference. I knew I'd found the right thing for me because when I visited those deaf schools, it made me feel *so* happy. Keep trying things until you find something that makes you feel like that. It might take a bit of time to find your cause, and that's totally fine.

Once you've found the thing you want to change, you have to work out how to make that change happen. I'm lucky that I can get my message out to lots of different people because I'm on *Gladiators*, but it wasn't always like that.

A great place to start is to speak to people who care about the same things as you.

YOU CAN HAVE MUCH MORE IMPACT IF YOU WORK AS PART OF A TEAM, INSTEAD OF ON YOUR OWN.

If there's an issue you really care about, you could set up a club at your school to work on change, or you could ask to speak in an assembly about it. I know that can be scary, and I was scared doing assemblies on my first school visits, but the feeling you get from it is amazing. I promise.

Tell as many people as possible about your cause, because you never know what could be sparked by even just one conversation. **We all have to start somewhere.** The more people you speak to, the more chances you have of making an impact. It can help to do some research into your cause as well so that you can share information about it.

When you really want to help people or change something, sometimes it can feel exhausting, because change usually happens slowly. **That's why it's really important to celebrate little wins along the way.** I haven't been able to teach every single person in the world about being deaf, and there are still loads of challenges out there for disabled people. But if I have a conversation that makes just one person a bit more understanding or knowledgeable about disabilities, that feels brilliant to me. Whatever you're aiming to change, you have to break it down into smaller, more manageable steps. And every time you get a step closer to where you want to be, take a moment to feel really proud of yourself — because you should!

Once you've found your cause, speak up about it and keep working hard to make the change you want to see. You might feel like you're one small person making little changes in the face of a big problem, but, over time, those little changes will make a big difference.

I KNOW YOU'VE GOT A FIRE INSIDE YOU AND I KNOW THAT FIRE IS SO POWERFUL.

Work out what makes your fire burn brighter, because you have the power to change the world.

ACTIVITIES

Here are some questions to ask yourself to help you find your cause and work out the best way to make change happen.

1 I felt like I had a fire inside me and I realized that working with disabled people and inspiring people to overcome barriers made it burn brighter. Close your eyes and take three deep breaths. Imagine there's a fire that's been lit in your belly. Sit for a few seconds and feel how powerful it is. What do you think would make your fire burn brighter? What do you really care about?

2 Having role models can inspire you to make change in the world. Who are your role models? What do you admire about them?

3 Is there something that you think is unfair in the world? What are three small steps you could take towards helping to change that thing? Who could support you to make that change? For example, you could ask your friends and family for help; you could do some reading about the topic and you could help others learn about it too.

4 Have you already worked to change something, maybe in your school or your community? What impact did that work have? What little wins do you want to celebrate?

CHAPTER 8

TRY AND TRY AGAIN

TRY

TRY

AGAIN

We've been through all the ups and downs of my life together in this book, and I'm guessing you've worked out by now that I've done a lot of things that have *terrified* me. I was really nervous standing up in front of my England teammates to tell them about being deaf. I was scared to try out for *Gladiators*. And those school visits I just told you about? So scary.

There have been lots of times in my life when trying something new has filled me with fear. And yet I've never regretted doing something scary. In fact, I've always been grateful I did.

You might have seen me on TV as Fury and think I'm naturally a really confident person. Gladiators aren't scared of anything, right? Well, you might be surprised to hear that when I was younger, I was so shy that I was scared to even go to the shops on my own.

I was always quite quiet with people I didn't know.
I would panic around new faces and not really
know what to say or how to start a conversation. In
restaurants, up until I was about fifteen, I'd be scared
to even ask for some ketchup to go with my chips!
And I'd get so worked up about going to
the shops to get milk – I was nervous
that I wouldn't be able to hear what
the person in the shop was saying, and
I'd hate the awkwardness of having to
explain that I hadn't heard them.

When I eventually learned how to be honest with people about my deafness, that really helped my confidence. But

that's something that's only happened in the past
few years. Before that, it was my parents who
supported me to keep trying, even when it was
scary. They encouraged me to step outside of my
comfort zone.

They pushed me: they told me that if I didn't go to the shop we just wouldn't have milk! If I wanted milk with my breakfast, I had to do the scary thing. And, amazingly, the more I did it, the less scary it became.

I realized that all the things I had worried about were never as bad as they seemed. You know the saying, practice makes perfect? That's true for scary things too. **When you practise doing the things you're scared of, they start to feel easier and less scary.**

When I was nine years old, I was competing at an athletics event and I met Linford Christie – he's this incredible Olympian who won 100-metre gold for Great Britain at the 1992 Olympics. I was in a 60-metre race and the other runners were a bit older than me, and I was so nervous because I felt so much smaller than everyone else. Linford Christie

walked past, and I think he could see that I was just full of nerves! I couldn't believe it when he actually stopped to talk to me.

He told me that . . .

Fourteen years later, I still think about that

... nerves are a good thing, because they show that you care about what you're doing.

all the time. When I'm nervous, I remind myself that it's a good thing. It means that whatever I'm doing is important to me. **It means I care about what happens next.**

There are *so* many times when pushing myself to do the thing I'm nervous about has worked out well for me. You remember how I'd begged my parents for months to let me play rugby? And we did all that research to find the best way for me to play with a cochlear implant? Once we'd got through all that, we'd found a scrum cap, we'd found a club, and then the day of my first training session arrived. As I sat in the car with my dad, waiting for the session to start, I suddenly thought, 'I can't do this.' It had just hit me.

I didn't know anyone else on the team. There would be loads of people there – new people – that I would have to talk to. I didn't know how to play rugby and I thought I was probably going to be really bad at it.

All these thoughts were swirling round my head and I was terrified. I turned to Dad and said, 'Can we just go home?'

My dad was brilliant. He reminded me of all the effort we'd put in to get to that point. He understood that trying new things can feel scary, but he said that if I just went for it, if I just walked into that practice, afterwards I would probably think, **'Why was I so stressed about that?'** Two girls walked past the car just then and they could see that I was scared. They asked if I wanted to walk to the rugby pitch with them, so I decided to just go for it. They were so welcoming and everyone was so lovely. Once I started playing, I remembered why I thought rugby looked so fun in the first place!

That was such an important moment in my life. I really thought I didn't have the confidence to go to that first rugby session. I'm so grateful to my dad for just giving me the little push I needed to take the leap and go for it. **Imagine if I hadn't done it! My life would look completely different now.** If I hadn't got out of the car that day I would never have played for England. I probably would never have had the opportunity to join *Gladiators*, and I wouldn't be talking to you now!

> SOMETIMES, WHEN YOU DON'T PUSH YOURSELF TO DO THINGS THAT SCARE YOU, YOU MISS OUT ON OPPORTUNITIES.

You have to take the leap into the unknown, because you never know which leap will completely change your life.

Of course, not every scary thing will have such a big impact. If you try something that you're really nervous about and you absolutely hate it, that's fine too. Then you've learned not to try it again! The important thing is that you're brave and you try anyway, because otherwise you'll never know where that opportunity might have led you. That's one of the things I love about the contenders on *Gladiators*. To me, *Gladiators* isn't about winning or losing. It's about the contenders having the courage to try and to give it their all, even though they're up against professional Gladiators who will be really hard to beat.

> # LIFE ISN'T ABOUT EVERYTHING GOING RIGHT ALL THE TIME; IT'S ABOUT WHAT YOU LEARN WHEN YOU'RE BRAVE ENOUGH TO GIVE THINGS A GO.

If you feel like you don't have the confidence to try new things or speak to new people, I understand. Sometimes I feel exactly the same. But being scared of something doesn't mean you should just never do it.

Do you know about comfort zones? Our comfort zone is the area where we feel really safe and cosy, where nothing scares us. That's a nice feeling, but we don't want to be in our comfort zones all the time.

THE MOST EXCITING CHANGES
IN OUR LIVES HAPPEN OUTSIDE
OUR COMFORT ZONES.

You can actually grow your comfort zone by trying new, scary things. When you try things that are outside your comfort zone, they often become less scary the more you do them. Eventually, when they're not scary any more, they become something that is *inside* your comfort zone and that means your comfort zone has grown bigger. But your comfort zone can shrink too. If you don't keep pushing at the edges of it by doing things that scare you, it might get smaller.

When you're growing your comfort zone, having confidence really helps. Confidence is something I've struggled with and I've had to work really hard at. I've picked up some tricks that hopefully will help you as much as they've helped me. With confidence, my motto is

FAKE IT 'TIL YOU MAKE IT.

Fake it 'til you make it means that sometimes, if you *act* like you're confident, it can actually make you *feel* confident. It's kind of like magic. I first heard the phrase when I was playing sevens for England. I've already told you that sevens is a really fast, tiring game. Our coaches taught us that if you show that you're really tired, maybe because you have your hands on your knees or you're on the floor trying to catch your breath, your opponents will see that and they will start to believe that it's easy to beat you. However, if you pretend that you're not tired, that you're actually really confident about winning and you stand up straight and look like you're ready to go, that will make your opponents nervous. So, even if I was absolutely exhausted and felt like I might fall over any minute, I'd present my body like I was ready to score a try. Then, when an opportunity came, I actually felt like I *was* ready and I believed I could score.

Now I do the same thing whenever I want to feel confident. When I have to talk in front of a big audience I try to stand in a way that makes me look confident. When I'm nervous I tend to curl up a bit and I play with my hands a lot. To look confident, I put my shoulders back and use my hands to help me express what I'm saying. I imagine I'm speaking to a friend, instead of a big room full of people.

PRESENTING MYSELF IN A CONFIDENT WAY ACTUALLY MAKES ME FEEL CONFIDENT.

Try it next time you're scared of doing something or you feel nervous.

BEFORE YOU KNOW IT, ACTING CONFIDENT WILL HELP YOUR CONFIDENCE GROW.

Asking people for feedback is really important, too, and I ask for it after I've done something that really scared me. Like those school visits I did when I was eighteen – afterwards I used to ask the teachers how they thought it went. After you do something that scares you it's easy to find negative thoughts in your head and to start thinking you were rubbish, but having feedback can help pull you out of that spiral. **The truth is, things are never as bad as you think.** Either people might say you did really well, which is great, or they might tell you ways that you can improve – and that is *so* useful because it shows you what you need to practise to do better next time!

Going on *Gladiators* for the first time definitely made me nervous. On the first day I went into the arena,

I saw the stage and thought, 'I can't believe I have to go up there!'. I didn't think I could do it. I'll let you in on a secret — one thing that's really helped me be confident on *Gladiators* is my Fury outfit. As soon as I see myself in the mirror with my Gladiator outfit and my Fury braids, my confidence switches on. When I'm scared I think,

and it helps me snap out of my fear. **Fury means business and she's fearless.** When I'm Fury, I know I can do anything.

I want you to embrace your Fury. Getting my Fury outfit on helps me do that. Obviously I'm not saying every time you try a scary thing you need to have a *Gladiators* outfit on, but try to find something that helps you get into your confident mode. I always find that if you feel good, you perform better. It could be a certain piece of clothing, a lucky piece of jewellery, a hairstyle or even a pair of socks. It doesn't have to be anything drastic, just a little something that helps you make that switch in your head, something that makes you think,

Today is my day.

I hope some of these ideas help you when you're trying new things. It took me years to build my confidence and there are always going to be things that scare me. **Feeling confident takes a lot of practice and it won't happen overnight.** I was scared to even go to the shop and speak to people when I was younger; now, I go on TV in front of huge audiences! Where we start out in life isn't necessarily where we have to end up.

WITH HARD WORK AND DETERMINATION, YOU CAN GROW.

You have to push your limits beyond what you thought was possible. When an opportunity comes your way, know that you are strong enough to give it a go, even if it's scary. Push yourself out of your comfort zone to get your biggest wins. Back yourself and throw yourself into things, even when you're afraid. Get comfortable with being uncomfortable; the more you do the uncomfortable things, the more comfortable they become. If you keep pushing yourself a bit further into the unknown whenever you can, eventually, when you look back you'll see how far you've come.

The main thing I really, *really* want you to take away from this book is to believe in yourself, even when it's scary. You might not get everything you want from life straight away, but the important thing is to keep taking those leaps into the unknown. Go for the things that you think will make you happy, because you deserve to have them. If things don't go your way at first, keep trying.

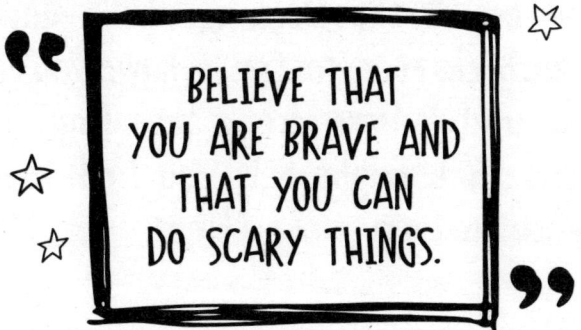

BELIEVE THAT
YOU ARE BRAVE AND
THAT YOU CAN
DO SCARY THINGS.

I am *so* proud of all the hard work you've put into your life so far and I know that if you back yourself, trust and believe in yourself, you are capable of anything.

I believe in you.
Go out there and smash it.

Jodie

ACTIVITIES

Good job on all the thinking you've done after each chapter so far. I hope you've found it useful! Here are a few final questions that might help you find your confidence and try new things.

I hope these questions help you to be confident, be brave and keep smashing it as you move through life. Just remember to back yourself. Amazing things can happen when you do.

1 **I used to be scared to go to the shops to buy milk, but I'm not any more. That's an example of my comfort zone growing. Can you think of something that used to feel really scary but that you now feel comfortable doing? What can you learn from that?**

2 If you're shy and feel nervous speaking to new people (like me), what are some small steps you can take to feel more confident? Which of the tips I shared on confidence feel like they could be useful to you? Are there any other ideas you have about things that could help make you feel more confident?

3 I was so nervous before my first rugby session, but once I tried it, I loved it! I was so glad I didn't give up. What is an example of something you were scared of at first, but were glad you'd done after? After thinking about that example, how do you feel about trying new things?

4 I really hope this book has helped you to find your dream and feel brave enough to chase it. Chasing your dream usually involves doing things that scare you. So, my final question to you is: to help you get your dream, what scary thing do you want to try next?

British Sign Language alphabet

British Sign Language numbers

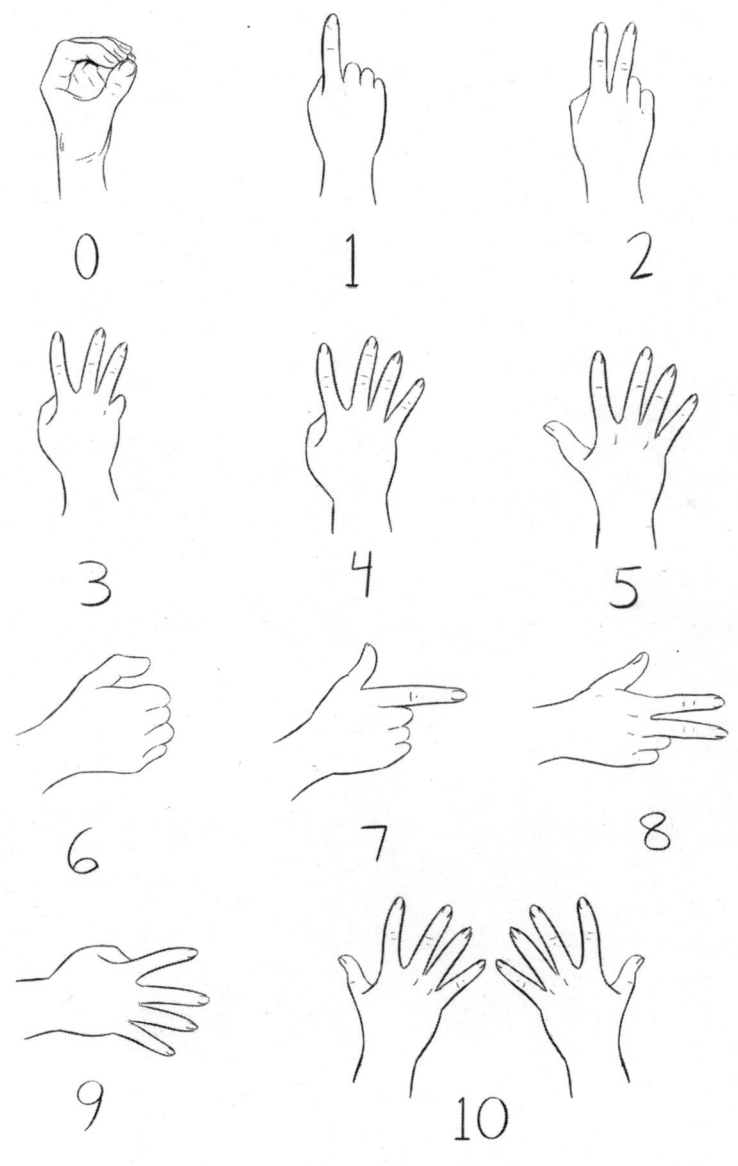

ABOUT THE AUTHORS

Jodie Ounsley is also known as being Fury from the BBC's *Gladiators*. She is a trailblazing British athlete, public speaker, and advocate for the deaf community. Born profoundly deaf, Jodie has defied the odds and shattered barriers to become a celebrated figure in sports and a role model for many. She became the first deaf female rugby player to play for a senior England side earning her first cap in 2019, and the first deaf player to represent on the sevens stage. Jodie is a patron of registered charity The Elizabeth Foundation. In 2020 Jodie won the Deaf Sports Personality of the Year award and, in 2023, was named Honorary President of UK Deaf Sport and included in the prestigious BBC Woman's Hour Women in Sport Power List. In 2024 she was a Paralympics C4 Broadcaster.

Keep Smashing It: Be Strong, Be Brave, Be Confident is her debut book, an inspirational guide-for-life to empower all children.

ABOUT THE AUTHORS

Becky Grey is a senior journalist at BBC Sport, who especially enjoys helping inspiring sportswomen tell their stories. Becky has worked at three Rugby World Cups, five Six Nations tournaments, the Commonwealth Games and Wimbledon. She co-produced BBC Elite British Sportswomen's Studies in 2020 and 2024, discussing the results on Woman's Hour and BBC Radio 5 Live. Outside of the BBC, Becky sits on the board of gender equity charity Queen Bee Coaching. Written with Jodie Ounsley, *Keep Smashing It: Be Strong, Be Brave, Be Confident* is her first book.

ABOUT THE ILLUSTRATOR

Dane Thibeault is a Canadian illustrator and designer. He has lived with severe hearing loss since the age of four which has impacted his life and communication.

His work has been published in children's books, magazines, and on a number of websites, and he loves creating both educational and entertaining content. He has illustrated a number of fiction and non-fiction children's books about animals, dinosaurs, and other scientific/historical topics. His editorial portrait illustration work has also been published in books and magazines, as well as the programme books for the Toronto Symphony Orchestra. He takes inspiration from science and history documentaries, classic storybook illustrations, fashion illustrations, and even music videos. In addition to collecting fountain pens and other art supplies, Dane enjoys collecting albums and listening to all different genres of music.

He lives in Calgary, Alberta, Canada.

ACKNOWLEDGEMENTS

First and foremost, If I could give the biggest and warmest hug through these pages to express my deepest gratitude, it would be for my mum and dad. Their unwavering support throughout this journey is beyond belief. They have done nothing but love me wholeheartedly and encourage me to dream big, whilst still always keeping me grounded.

Thank you to my No. 1 supporters, Grandad Rog and Dee, I am incredibly grateful for you being my cheerleaders literally EVERYWHERE I go, even when we are half the world away from each other. For inspiring me and fuelling my determination to overcome any barriers and challenges sent my way, I'd like to thank and pay tribute to Auntie Jane and Granny, two very special women in my life. Special thanks to my agent, Claire Donald, who is not only an incredible agent but has also become a true friend and huge part of the Ounsley family.

This book would have not been possible without Becky Grey. She magically understood me and our chats turned into hours of what felt like therapy! She has brought my story to life in the most raw and beautiful way, I am honoured and grateful to have written this with her. To Lydia and Becca, my book agents at Darley Anderson Children's, thank you for believing in me. You have helped myself and Claire navigate this crazy new world, I couldn't imagine doing this with any other team.

Finally, I'd like to extend my appreciation to the amazing team at Macmillan. From the very first call, it felt like the right home for me and this book, thank you.

ETERNAL CHAMPIONS *Adventure Gamebook 1*:
CITADEL OF CHAOS
Jamie Thompson

In the world of the far future, the forces of evil
technology threaten to take over. The spirit of mankind
has been sapped. Only the Eternal Champion has the
power to change history by summoning heroes from
the past.

The battle with the forces of evil has now reached new
heights. You have received the call to take your place
with the world's greatest martial arts heroes. Your
mission is seemingly impossible – to penetrate and
capture a hostile citadel.

ETERNAL CHAMPIONS *Adventure Gamebook 2*:
THE CYBER WARRIORS
Jamie Thompson

The time is in the far future. Technology has taken over
and mankind lives a miserable existence. Only the
Eternal Champion has the power to restore the balance
between Good and Evil. To do this he needs to call upon
the skill and bravery of the world's greatest martial arts
heroes from the past.

You have received the call of destiny from the Eternal
Champion. Your task is to take on the evil Overlord who
has sent cybernetic replicas of those martial arts heroes
into the past. Unless you intervene, the future will be
ruined and mankind destroyed.